THE
EDITOR

THE
EDITOR

By

Luke Carroll

**ANT COLONY
PRESS**

Ant Colony Press, a division of Olive Group, LLC,
P.O. Box 1577, Belton, MO 64012

ISBN-13: 978-1720662822

Ant Colony Press 1st edition June 2018

10 9 8 7 6 5 4 3 2 1

Manufactured in the United States of America

For information regarding special discounts for bulk purchases, please contact Ant Colony Press at antcolonypress@gmail.com.

www.antcolonypress.com

This is for my Dad.
Your love of reading encouraged me to write.
And for my daughters.
Your love of reading continues to motivate me.
Love you, love you, buddies.

October 25th, 2016

Pittsburgh, Pennsylvania – Strip District

Lincoln Larkin stumbles into the damp, murky alley between Hobe's—his third favorite pub—and the coffee shop next door, looking for a place to expel tonight's overindulgence of Blanton's. It's become a nightly ritual that he uses to drown his misery. He acquired the expensive taste when things were better, when his name was on the New York Times Bestseller list. Now that he's basically living off royalties, he should probably drink from a lower shelf, but he can't seem to stomach much else.

As he makes his way further into the narrow abyss his nausea is suddenly intensified by the smell of blood that hangs thick in the air, seemingly one with the fog. He's sure it's just his imagination, but a wave of déjà vu washes over him. It's almost as if he has walked into one of the shoddiest stories that he'd ever written.

"Really? It had to be *Vriends*?" His drunken laugh echoes down the alley. He assumes the bourbon's got the best of him and that he's now in the midst of a vivid dream.

Some of his better works originated from these dreams, so it's extremely disappointing to dream about a failed story like this one. As he continues to feel his way down the alley, he thinks about what a dumb idea the spoof had been. Vampires who gain special powers by drinking only caffeinated blood—it was bad enough the first time, he certainly didn't need to relive it in his dreams.

As his gait becomes increasingly wobbly, he steps into a puddle of warm liquid that covers his sandaled feet. He scrambles to find the flashlight app on his phone when a somewhat familiar laugh echoes off the alley walls. He glances up in time to see the tail end of a figure disappear around the back of the building. He runs as fast as a drunken man in sandals can run, but by the time he covers the fifteen yards to where the figure disappeared, no one is in sight.

"I need to stop drinking." He rubs his eyes before going back to his phone and finally turning on the flashlight and shining it over his feet. "Aw, what the...?"

"That'll teach you to wear sandals in the fall."

The voice sends chills down his spine, and before he can turn to find its source, there is a pinch at his neck followed by a burning sensation. Just as the lightheadedness begins to set in, the burning abruptly stops.

"Come on, man! When's the last time you had a decent cup of coffee?"

Before Lincoln can even begin to formulate a reply, the man disappears, seemingly into thin air.

Lincoln chuckles as he makes his way back into the bar. "Nope, I was wrong. I need to drink more."

Chapter 1

October 27th, 2016 Pittsburgh, Pennsylvania
South Side District

Eddie Chamberlain opens his eyes for what seems like the first time. An aching thirst that he cannot explain intensifies by the second. He scans the room, which is somehow familiar to him, although he doesn't remember where he is or how he got there. The room is sparsely furnished. There's the queen four-post bed that he woke up on, an ornate dresser with a small television on top, an oversized chair on the far wall, and a small end table next to the bed. He notices a bottle of Eagle Rare on the bedside table and pours himself three fingers worth. As he swallows his first sip and relishes the smooth taste, the thirst begins to dissipate and he feels his body begin to strengthen.

Eddie makes his way to the door and opens it cautiously. He doesn't feel any real sense of danger—rather, an odd sense of home—but he still can't shake the butterflies from his stomach. The door opens into the rest of the apartment, which is more modernly decorated, but it's obvious to him that this is the home of a bachelor; the lack of pictures and color make this evident. One wall is made up completely of windows and Eddie makes his way there to try to get a better feel for where he is.

Outside is a cold, hard city. The buildings vary in size, but are mostly brick or stone with a few steel sky-scrapers mixed in between. In the distance is a bridge with a fair amount of traffic on it, stretching over a river. Closer, people scurry through the streets, trying to avoid the brisk autumn breeze. As another mouth-ful of the bourbon finds the back of his throat, a toilet flushes. He whirls around with catlike reflexes to find a wide-eyed man staring back at him.

"Oh, Eddie. Good, you're up." The man takes a step toward him.

He looks tired, but not helpless, so Eddie tenses for a fight. The man, like the apartment, looks familiar, as though he were a relative that he hadn't seen since childhood. He has dark hair and dark eyes, not unlike Eddie's, but this man's hair and beard are long and unkempt, two things that Eddie could never tolerate.

The man pauses, likely noticing the bewildered look on Eddie's face. "Right... you have no idea who I am. Lincoln Larkin," he says as he extends a hand. "I created you."

Chapter 2

"Ah, and I see you found your bourbon, too. Very good." Lincoln sits down in front of a laptop at a glass-top desk with cinder blocks for legs. The desk faces the windows at the far side of the room.

"Can we back up to the *you created me* stuff?"

Lincoln grins knowingly and nods. "I know this is all kinda hard to believe, but I can explain."

"Are you trying to tell me that *you're* God?"

Lincoln lowers his head and mumbles, "Far from it."

Eddie scoffs at Lincoln before he prods further. "Okay, let me analyze this. *I'm* thirty-five. *You* can't be much older. *I've* traveled the world, am fluent in three languages, have a Master belt in Tang Soo Do, and can run a six-minute mile without any difficulty. *You* look like you haven't left this apartment in years, probably haven't talked to anyone—besides me—in at least as long, and I doubt you can make it downstairs without getting winded. Explain to me how someone like *you* created someone like *me*?"

The Editor

Lincoln begins to speak, but is unable to get a word out before Eddie cuts him off. "I mean, no offense, but shouldn't a *creator* be better than his creation?"

Lincoln chuckles at the last statement and pours Eddie another glass of bourbon before he speaks. "First, you should be able to run a *five*-minute mile," he says curiously. "Must have been a typo," he mutters under his breath.

"The answer to your last question is... complicated. You're different from any of my other creations. For reasons that I'll do my best to explain, I had to make you an extension of myself. A better version, if you will."

"So, you're telling me that I'm you, just better?" Eddie rolls his eyes, but somehow knows it to be true.

"Pretty much. Watch this. Think of anything you want and I'll tell you what you're thinking. We have this... sort of... connection."

"*Riiiight*. Okay, weirdo. I'll play your game. What am I thinking?" Eddie imagines a hot blonde woman bringing him a pizza.

"You're hungry." Lincoln shifts his eyes to the ground momentarily. "And horny." He blushes as he watches Eddie's eyes grow wide and notices a small gasp before he quickly recovers his composure.

Eddie shrugs. "Okay, but you also just described most any male my age."

"True, but I have an idea. Let's go and grab you somethin' to eat and I'll communicate the rest of my explanation to you without speaking out loud. I know a great pizza place with a beautiful blonde bartender that I think you'll like."

Chapter 3

Eddie follows Lincoln out of the apartment and down a dirty alley. The wind whips between the buildings and straight into Eddie's face.

It's even colder than it looked, he thinks.

"Thick beard helps this time of year." Lincoln chuckles as he puts his head down and picks up the pace.

They make a left onto Sarah Street and walk for two blocks. Everything seems completely familiar to Eddie: the row houses with the pubs tucked in between them, the sound of angry commuters honking at tourists looking for a place to park, and even the smell of bratwurst and beer as they pass college students grilling on their front stoop before the weekly football game. Without even noticing, he opens the door to Michael's restaurant for Lincoln.

"Ah, I see you know the place as well." Lincoln winks. Eddie ignores Lincoln, but realizes that he isn't sure how he knew where they were going. His head spins. Again, the place seems oddly familiar to him, although he's sure that he's never been there before.

The restaurant is really more of a bar with a few tables for dining. It's small, but homey and warm, the type of place that you could go every day without getting tired of it. It has a small-town feel despite its location in the center of the city. The décor isn't fancy, but every piece has meaning—from the autographed picture of Mean Joe Greene, to the portrait of Michael Keaton, down to the garden gnome wearing a Pirates jersey. Somehow it all just goes together.

Now take a seat at the corner table. We wouldn't want anyone getting too suspicious of our nonverbal conversation.

"Did you just speak to me from inside my own head?" Eddie whispers as they sit down at the table.

Lincoln smirks. *Yep. And you can do it too. You just have to make a conscious effort.*

"Okay, let me try." Eddie places his fingers on his temples and closes his eyes. *Eaaaat SHIIIIT!*

Real nice, Eddie. And you don't have to yell. Why don't you just sit back and order a pizza. Ogle Beth and let me explain.

The attractive bartender walks over to the table and flashes a seductive smile. Her shoulder-length blonde hair is pulled back in a ponytail, and although her weary eyes are those of an overworked middle-aged housewife, she has the tight body of a much younger woman.

"Hey, Lincoln! How's the book coming?" She sounds genuinely interested, but her eyes keep shifting to Eddie.

"Oh, uh, well, this one's kind of writing itself, I guess." He smiles weakly.

"And who's this? A cousin? You guys sorta look alike, except, well, he's, uh..." Color floods Beth's cheeks as she stammers, looking for the right words.

"This is my, um...this is Eddie. Eddie, meet Beth. She's the best bartender, waitress, yoga instructor, and soon-to-be lawyer in Pittsburgh."

"Consider me impressed." Eddie takes Beth's outstretched hand and gently kisses the back of it, causing the recently departed color to return to her cheeks.

"Well, what'll it be, boys?" Beth bats her eyes, obviously smitten with Eddie.

"A large cheese pizza, an order of fries, two bourbons, and another one of those smiles." Eddie flashes a smile of his own. "And whatever he wants."

I told you she was cute.

Eddie ignores Lincoln's thoughts as his eyes meet Beth's once more before she leaves the table. As she walks away, he thinks about what a personal yoga lesson with Beth would be like.

Lincoln runs his hand through his unkempt hair. *Unreal. I provide an extremely complimentary introduction and she doesn't even thank me. You kiss her hand and she practically has to change her panties. And stop thinking about her like that. I hear EVERYTHING you're thinking right now.*

Well, maybe you should have thought of that before you "created" me. Does sarcasm transfer in mind-speak? Eddie leans back, chuckling out loud.

Yes, and people are going to think you're crazy if you keep laughing when we haven't spoken a word out loud yet. Lincoln glares at Eddie before he quickly scans each person in the bar, trying to gauge if anyone noticed Eddie's odd behavior.

"Thanks, Beth." Eddie flashes another smile as the bartender places his glasses of bourbon in front of him. She puts a gentle hand on his shoulder and makes sure to squeeze past him, brushing slightly against his arm as she places Lincoln's raspberry iced tea in front of him.

Okay then, Lincoln. I'm going to sit back, sip some bourbon and watch the game. Eddie glances at the TV, where Beth just put a football game on. *Feel free to explain away.*

Chapter 4

Lincoln sits back in his chair and takes a sip of his tea. Alright then, here it goes. I'm an author. A hack, really. I had one huge hit series when I was still in college, but haven't had anything good published in a decade. I've been writing pop-culture spoofs, rewriting other people's stories, and even writing teeny-bopper fan fiction.

Eddie rolls his eyes. *Look, I'm thoroughly enjoying your self-deprecating life story here, but get to the point.*

Okay, okay. So, I've been writing these crap books, right? Now, all of a sudden, some of my characters are showing up in the real world. You may wonder how I could possibly know this, or why no one else has noticed.

Eddie rolls his eyes again, but then starts to smile as Beth approaches with the pizza and Lincoln's black bean burger. "Pizza, fries, bourbon, and Beth. This must be Heaven!"

Beth blushes again. "You keep talking like that and I might just take you home with me." Her playful laugh causes Lincoln to choke on his first bite of burger.

Without hesitation, Eddie springs to his feet and slaps Lincoln's back, dislodging the food.

"Thanks," Lincoln manages after a few mouthfuls of tea. The rest of the people in the bar, who had temporarily put their drunken ramblings on hold, return to their own conversations, but Beth stays at the table.

"My hero!" She laughs playfully again. "In all seriousness though, you did save my best frie—customer." She smiles kindly at Lincoln, then kisses Eddie softly on the cheek and whispers, "I'm done at eleven if you want to hang out later."

Eddie doesn't take his eyes off her as she walks back to the bar.

"I'm fine by the way," Lincoln calls out after Beth.

Well, that's one way not to draw attention to us. Eddie thinks back as he glares impatiently at Lincoln. *Finish your story before Beth gets off work.*

Lincoln scowls and picks at his fries. Eddie pretends not to notice and goes back to watching the game.

Where was I? Ah yes, how do I know my characters are coming to life and why doesn't anyone else notice? Most of my novels are based in or around the Pittsburgh area. Crimes that I wrote about are starting to happen. At first, I thought it to be a coincidence, or that a fan of my writing was trying to portray my characters. But when I saw things from some of my unpublished novels

22

starting to happen, I got more curious. I went places where I knew my characters would go and I watched them. I saw them doing things that real people couldn't do, yet there they were—real people. Then, the other night, well...

So now I'm not even real? Come on buddy, this is some crazy shit you're trying to sell me. Eddie interjects, not letting Lincoln complete his thought.

Oh, you're very real now, but you weren't yesterday until I wrote your back-story. I know you're skeptical, as well you should be, but humor me. Take a sip of your bourbon.

Eddie eyes his glass before lifting it in a mock toast. "Cheers!" He swallows a mouthful of his Blanton's and stares across the table at Lincoln.

Now look at the asshole at the bar trying to grope Beth and think...

Eddie snaps his head around to see the perpetrator and suddenly the man's barstool gives way, causing the man to fall embarrassingly to the ground. Subsequently, the bouncer begins to escort the man from the bar.

Now you're going to tell me I did that with my mind, huh? Eddie retorts.

Yep. Go ahead, try something else.

Eddie thinks about the man tripping on his way out and almost instantaneously, the man faceplants in front of a couple college kids who greet him with a round of applause. The man tries to explain that he only had two beers, but the bouncer will have none of it, and closes the door behind him.

"So, I can control things with my mind?" Eddie leans in and whispers, still sounding a bit skeptical.

Lincoln shrugs. "As long as you have bourbon, you can do whatever it takes to defeat your nearest enemy."

"You act like that's a normal thing to say to somebody," Eddie replies through gritted teeth. "Okay, so even if this is true, why wouldn't you just give me the powers outright? Why would you make me rely on bourbon? Not that I'm complaining." Eddie's voice is a little too loud, and one of the college kids raises an eyebrow. Lincoln kicks him under the table.

Come on, Eddie. Use the damn mind-speak. As for the bourbon, I guess that's the author in me. I had to make you a little more interesting. Anti-heroes are all the rage now, so I had to give you your flaws.

Flaws? The plural form of the word catches Eddie's attention.

Yes, you may have a few other addictions, too. Lincoln glances towards Beth as he takes another bite of his burger.

The Editor

Okay man, that's about all the bullshit I can take at the moment. Why don't you slip me a hundred, get a take-home container, and head back to the apartment? I'll be home... later. Eddie gazes at the beautiful bartender.

"I'm done, anyway. Not much of an appetite anymore. Just be back in the morning. We have a lot more to discuss." Lincoln pushes his chair back from the table, waves a friendly goodbye to Beth, and heads back to the apartment.

"Hey, wait, the mon—" Eddie starts to call after him.

We eat for free here. Enjoy your night, Eddie. Tomorrow may not be as fun.

Chapter 5

Lincoln's alarm sounds at five thirty just as it does every day. Despite the late nights and the copious amounts of booze, he's always been an early riser. He drags himself out of bed and fumbles through his cupboards looking for a K-Cup to pop in his seldom used Keurig. He hasn't had to brew an actual pot of coffee since Beth left him four years ago. For the past two years, he's been finishing the previous night's bourbon each morning, but in light of recent events, he's decided that he needs to keep his head as clear as possible. Eddie still has not returned, so he turns on the television to catch the local news.

The top story is about mysterious deaths on back-to-back nights at a local coffee shop.

"It can't be." Lincoln runs both hands through his hair and down to the back of his neck.

"It can't be what?" Eddie says as he swings the door open.

The Editor

Lincoln glances at Eddie and notices the smug grin on his face before turning back to the TV. "Quiet. I need to hear this."

Eddie continues into the apartment, picks Lincoln up, and twirls him around. "It's hard to be quiet when you're in love!" He sings.

Lincoln can smell Beth's perfume mixed with a myriad of other not-so-pleasant scents. "Put me down, Eddie."

Eddie does as he is told this time. "What crawled up your ass?"

"Let's just get one thing clear. I brought you into this world and I can take you out of it at any time. Now go get some rest, or at least a shower, so we can start saving the city."

Chapter 6

It's about twelve thirty in the afternoon when Eddie finally makes his way back out to the living room. He finds Lincoln on the couch scouring the Internet news and gossip sites.

"What are you looking for?" Eddie yawns and wipes the sleep from his eyes.

Lincoln doesn't even look up, but instead flicks his hand to the left towards a glass of Eagle Rare that he had waiting for Eddie on the kitchen island. Eddie grabs the glass and swallows it in two gulps.

"What'd I do to you, man? I didn't mean to piss in your Cheerios. I'm sorry I came in so late. We just had a great time. I didn't—"

Lincoln waves at Eddie dismissively. "It's nothing. Don't worry about it. Just come over here so I can finish explaining. We'll need to get to work faster than I thought."

Eddie sits down next to Lincoln on what appears to be an extremely expensive white leather couch.

Lincoln reads his thoughts and responds. "Like I said, I had one series of books that was *extremely* successful. The royalties still allow me to live comfortably."

Eddie nods as if he's impressed. "Okay, so let's pretend for a minute that I believe your whole story. Why'd you create me? I mean, was it just for shits and giggles or did you have a purpose for me?"

Lincoln doesn't answer but turns his laptop around so that Eddie can see the screen. It's a tabloid site and the headline reads, "Coffee Shop Vampire Strikes Again— Time for Some Decaf."

"Oh, that's bad." Eddie's face tenses as if he just ate something sour.

Lincoln nods solemnly.

"Tell me you didn't write that."

"Damnit, Eddie! This is serious. Last year I wrote a spoof of a once-popular sitcom about six friends who hung out in a coffee shop. I made all the friends vampires, but not your run-of-the-mill, *any blood will do* vampires; these vampires had to have caffeinated blood to survive."

Eddie bursts into raucous laughter. "What is it with you and drinks?"

Lincoln fights to hold back a smile of his own. "I don't know, but it's probably why I haven't been published in years. Listen to me, though, Eddie. These vampires are no joke. I made their need for caffeine into both a weakness and a strength. It allows them to be stronger than normal—fictional—vampires and gives them other supernatural powers. They can't be killed by wood, silver has no effect on them, nor does holy water, garlic, sunlight, or fire. They can be killed three ways: by removal of both their head and their heart, by stakes made of pure ivory, or finally by a—" Lincoln pauses and color rushes to his cheeks.

"A what?" Eddie leans in eagerly.

"A decaf enema."

Eddie falls over on the arm of the couch and laughs until tears roll down his face. "This is hilarious, man. You want me to stroll into a coffee shop, drop a vampire's pants, and give him a decaf enema? It's a wonder you don't have Pulitzer's all over this place. I'm heading back over to Beth's before her shift starts."

Eddie gets up from the couch and takes two steps towards the door. He hears Lincoln tap a few keys on the laptop and suddenly his legs give out. Eddie can feel his heart beat in his ears and is starting to find it hard to breathe. "What the hell, man? I can't feel my legs!" He grabs at his legs frantically as he looks back at Lincoln.

"Like I said. I can erase you at any moment. Right

now, I decided that you may be more interesting as a paraplegic."

"Not funny, man." Eddie crawls back toward the couch. "Okay, I'll kill your lame ass vampires, just make my legs work," he pleads.

With a few more keystrokes, Eddie feels the life begin to return to his legs. He gets back to his feet and slams his fist into the side of Lincoln's face. "Never again. Understand?" He speaks calmly as Lincoln slowly recovers from the blow. "Why don't you just do that stuff to the vampires? Kill them with your computer."

"I tried. I couldn't update any characters that were already... alive. So, when I made you, I wrote it into your story that I, and only I, could update you."

"Lucky me," Eddie scoffs.

Lincoln rubs the left side of his jaw. "There's a bag in your closet. It has what you'll need in it. The coffee shop is on Sarah Street around the 28th street intersection. Use the mind-speak to communicate with me and get a bourbon on the way." Lincoln holds his glass of iced tea up to the side of his face. "If you're lucky, I'll let you have the full use of your body when you get back."

Chapter 7

Eddie stops at a dive bar on his way to the coffee shop. It's literally no more than a long bar inside, no tables or anything. It's decorated like a trendy upscale hotel bar and is probably a popular spot for some of the local professionals to stop on their way home from work. Right now it's empty with the exception of him and the bartender, an older man, probably in his late fifties.

"What'll it be, bud?" The man tosses a towel that he'd been using to dry beer glasses into the sink, semi-annoyed that he has to stop watching *The Ellen Show*.

"A bourbon on ice. Make it a double."

The bartender pours some Knob Creek over ice and Eddie sips it while they finish watching *Ellen* together, mostly in comfortable silence. She gives a couple high school kids money for college because they created an anti-bullying app.

"This show always gives me the feels." The bartender quickly wipes a lone tear from his cheek.

Eddie shuffles in his seat, not really knowing how to react to the man's tears. "Yeah; if more people showed that sort of kindness, we'd all be much better off," Eddie replies sincerely. "Well, I better head out; I gotta couple coffee-loving vampires to kill."

The bartender raises one eyebrow, then starts to laugh. "I like you, man. Name's Lukas." He extends a bear paw of a hand.

"Eddie Chamberlain. I'm sure we'll be seein' plenty of each other." Eddie swallows the last of his bourbon and hands Lukas the glass. He reaches into his wallet and is surprised to see that it's full of cash. *Where'd this come from?*

In your story, you're paid handsomely to do your jobs by a rich benefactor. Don't get any big ideas, though. You'll only ever have what you need and no more.

Eddie hands Lukas a twenty and heads outside. *Get out of my head, Lincoln. I'll let you know when I need you.*

Chapter 8

The sun has started to fade behind the city sky-line and the wind whips cruelly between the buildings. Eddie zips his Carhart jacket and shoves his hands in the pockets. He feels inside his pocket and pulls out a black ski cap that he quickly stretches over his head.

He makes his way down the street past many res-taurants and many more people, none of which seem extraordinary. He spies the sign for the coffee shop on the next block and picks up his pace. As he opens the door to *South Side Perk* and steps inside, a couple of giggling college-age women breeze past him and smile. He's not sure if they were flirting with him or laughing at him because he sticks out like a sore thumb in this place.

Eddie opens the mental connection with Lincoln. *Okay, I'm in.*

Good. Act normal but scan the place and tell me what you see, Lincoln instructs.

Act normal? You made me a drunken womanizer. Coffee shops aren't my normal hangout.

Just order something. Lincoln taps a few keys on his laptop. *Try a caramel macchiato. You'll like it.*

Eddie scans the faces in the shop as he gets in line to order his "caramel macchiato."

There are a couple hacker types in the back—probably stealing credit card information or something—a mom and a little girl in front of me, the barista, a dorky guy and his jock friend sitting on a couch. The jock just tried to hit on the mom in an annoyingly stereotypical Italian-American accent. She shot him down—it was actually quite entertaining.

No attractive women with the dork and jock?

Nah. The mom is a milf, but there's no other women in here but the barista. Two cute girls left as I was coming in, but—

What did they look like?

I don't know, man. They were pretty bundled up. One was a taller blonde and the other had jet-black hair. I think the blonde called her Courtney.

That was two of the women! Lisa and Courtney. Were they following anyone?

Not that I saw. No one else left the shop as I was walking up the block.

Okay. The dork and jock are most likely David and Matt. When you get your coffee, sit down next to them and say, "Dave and Matt, right?"

Dude, your plans are the worst. These two are just a couple schmucks who have nothing better to do than hang out here—ogling moms in yoga pants—from the looks of it.

"I'll have a small caramel macchiato, please." Eddie's awkward delivery brings a wide smile to the barista's face. Her name tag says "June" and she's a young girl with brown hair, probably in high school. She's thin, but with a basketball-shaped protrusion under her apron. Eddie makes a mental note to give her a big tip.

"You want whipped cream on that, big fella?"

Eddie chuckles at her sarcasm and shakes his head. He turns back around to check on the bromance that was David and Matt, but both men are gone. Then he hears the blood-curdling scream.

Shit!

What? Shit—what?!

June, remembering what happened outside the shop a few days earlier, starts to tremble. Pools begin to form in each of her big, brown eyes as she looks towards the back of the shop.

"June, is there an exit back there? Did the mom and little girl go out that way?"

June nods her head as the tears begin to spill down her cheeks.

The Editor

Eddie races towards the back door and kicks it open just in time to see David and Matt each with their teeth sunk deep into one side of the mother's neck. The little girl stands against a wall in the alley screaming at the top of her lungs.

Eddie reaches into his coat and grabs an ivory stake. He feels his vision begin to sharpen and his muscles begin to bulge. He hurls the stake toward David, the closer of the two, and it pierces the vampire just to the left of his spine. The little girl shrieks again as David releases his hold on her mother and disintegrates before her eyes.

Matt, eyes wide and mouth agape, drops the woman's lifeless body and turns to run. The vampire is fast—unearthly fast— but Eddie is faster. He catches Matt by the collar and flings him—as if he were nothing more than an empty beer bottle—against a nearby building, knocking the mortar between a few of the bricks loose. He has no idea where they are but he hears running water, which must be coming from the other side of the train tracks that he now stands next to. They must have run ten blocks, and he's thankful that there is no one around to watch what's unfolding.

Eddie stalks toward Matt, who's rubbing the back of his head while trying to get back to his feet.

Rip his heart out, Eddie.

Eddie picks the vampire up by his neck as if he were a doll. Suddenly the vampire's body begins to harden, forming an almost stone-like shell.

What the—? He just turned to stone.

It's okay, rip his heart out, Eddie.

Eddie shakes his head and drives his fist into Matt's chest cavity, easily breaking the vampire's torso into gravel and surprising himself at the same time. He feels around until he clenches the beast's slowly beating heart. Eddie raises an eyebrow. "It beats?"

"How *you* doin'... this?" It's all the vampire can say before Eddie tears out his heart and tosses it into the nearby river. Then, remembering Lincoln's initial instructions, he rips the head from the body— with as much effort as it takes a normal person to remove the foil seal on a can of Pringles— and discards it in the same way.

Two down.

Chapter 9

Eddie races back to the alley behind the coffee shop where he finds June trying to console the little girl who is sobbing over the lifeless body of her mother.

"I'm sorry," Eddie whispers inaudibly.

June looks up and wipes the tears from her cheeks as she senses him there. "Where did *you* come from? And why are you covered in bloo—" she begins to ask angrily before she realizes what happened.

She pulls Eddie aside so that the little girl can't hear their conversation. "Noooo shit. You're some kind of vampire slayer or somethin', huh?"

Eddie kicks at some stones, ignoring the question. "How's the girl?"

"Not exactly MENSA though, I see. Her mom just died in front of her, Einstein. How do you think she is? Help me get her inside."

Eddie scoops the girl up in his arms and carries her inside. "Listen, June. I can't be here when the cops show up. You get that, right?"

June nods. "Okay, but you have to take her. If she tells them that she saw vampires attack her mom until a man with glowing eyes showed up and fought them off, they'll think she's *Looney Toons.*"

"Glowing eyes?"

"Yeah, dude. You are in full-on werewolf mode right now." June motions to a mirror on the wall to his right.

Eddie turns toward the mirror where two eyes that not only glow, but seem to emit a white light, stare back at him. "Holy—"

"Exactly." June laughs. "I would have said archangel or something, but I could smell the bourbon before you even walked in."

Eddie chuckles. "What? You don't think angels drink from rivers of bourbon in Heaven?" He looks back over his shoulder at the crying child. "So, what am I supposed to do with a little girl?"

"Wait. You aren't some kind of creep or something, are you?"

"What? Um... no. Of course not!"

"Easy, big fella. I'm just messin' with ya. Just take her to Michael's. It's a bar a few blocks—"

"Yeah, I know it," Eddie nods and scoops the still-sobbing little girl up into his arms.

The Editor

June smirks. "Of course you do. Well, her aunt works there. I think her name is Beth."

Chapter 10

"Oh my God! Noel! Eddie! What happened?" Beth shrieks as Eddie walks into Michael's carrying the little girl. Her crying has slowed but not completely stopped.

"Eddie? What's going...? Where's Sara?"

"I... I don't..." Eddie hangs his head. Sara must be the girl's mother; Beth's sister.

"Noel, sweetie, where is mommy?" Beth pleads with her niece as Eddie notices a scowling man approaching.

"Beth! I've told you for the last time not to bring this shit in here. Whose kid is this and why is she covered in blood?" He seems to finally notice the tears that have welled up in Beth's eyes. "Take it outside. I can't have it ruining my business."

Beth scoops up Noel and carries her out into the street.

"Seriously? The kid just watched her mom die and you kick her out in the cold?" Eddie feels his muscles begin to swell again, although he hardly thinks the extra strength will be necessary for him to pummel this jerk.

The man's eyes grow wide at the sight of Eddie transforming. "Oh. I...I didn't know..."

"Exactly. You didn't know. You also didn't bother to ask. That's why I'm telling you. I'm also telling you that Beth will have the rest of the week off—paid—and you'll work her shifts and give her the tips. Got it, boss?" Eddie stares into the jerk's eyes and is met only with a nod confirming that everything he demanded will come to fruition.

"Nice. Hopefully we didn't *ruin your business* too much." Eddie takes a quick step in his direction, causing him to stumble back against a chair, drawing a laugh from some of the customers. Then he turns and heads out to help Beth with Noel. As he opens the door, he hears the customers inside start to clap and heckle Beth's jerk of a manager.

Chapter 11

"Come on. Let's get her somewhere safe and warm." Eddie takes Noel from Beth's arms and follows her down a damp, dark alley next to the bar that leads to an old schoolhouse that has now been converted into an apartment building. They take a marble staircase to the second floor and walk down the narrow corridor until they reach the last door on the right—Beth's apartment. Eddie vaguely remembers it from the previous night.

Noel has cried herself to sleep in Eddie's arms so he gently lays her down on Beth's bed. There's an afghan hanging on a nearby chair. He grabs it and uses it to cover the sleeping child.

Yeah, on top of the sheets is the safer play. He thinks back to his and Beth's previous night together.

Ah! Come on, man! Lincoln shoots back in mindspeak as Eddie makes his way out to Beth's couch.

Sorry Lincoln, but why are you so offended by the thought of Beth and me? Oh.

Before Lincoln can reply, Beth hands Eddie a mug and smiles sadly. "Hot chocolate?" Eddie can sense tears are about to come, so instead of telling the truth that he despises hot chocolate, he swallows a mouthful and smiles warmly.

"Mmmm. Just what I needed," he offers back with a weak grin. "So, do you want me to call Noel's dad?"

"That deadbeat? No."

"Okay, but deadbeat or not, the police will eventually notify him. I'm sure he'd like to—"

"Honestly, I have no idea who it is. Sara got pregnant by accident. We told each other everything, but she would never tell me who the father was, just that she was going to do the right thing and have the baby. I didn't want to push it, so I just decided to be the best aunt I could be. I assumed that Sara would eventually get married and Noel would have a dad, but..." Beth takes a drink of her hot chocolate and grimaces. "Shit! How did you swallow this stuff?"

Eddie wonders the same thing and attributes it to his superpowers, so he decides to only tell a half-lie. "I had some not-so-smooth bourbon earlier; nothing burns compared to that." He chuckles and Beth smirks too. His smile widens as he relaxes deeper into the couch cushions. "Hey, so your boss said you could have the rest of the week off—paid—and he would give you all the tips he makes covering your shifts."

Beth raises her eyebrows. "That doesn't sound like Bobby. I was sure I was fired."

"Yeah, well, Bobby is turning over a new leaf." Eddie forces down the last of his hot chocolate.

Beth looks at him, still wondering how he's drinking it, and their eyes meet.

To Eddie, she looks so fragile, yet so beautiful. *I need to leave. I don't want to take advantage of her in this state.*

Good idea.

For real, Lincoln. I don't need you in my head right now.

It's not by choice, believe me. You need to get better at controlling what you share.

"Beth, is there anything I can get you before I go?" Eddie puts his hand on her knee which is exposed through a rip in her jeans.

"Can you stay the night?" she pleads meekly. "I think the morning is going to be bad."

Eddie considers her request. He can't say no to her. "Sure, but I need to get you into your room with Noel and then go home to shower and change. I don't think Noel needs to see me covered with blood first thing in the morning. Then I'll come back and sleep on the couch. Okay?"

Beth nods reluctantly. "Just hurry back. Please." She hands Eddie a spare key to her apartment before he tucks her in next to Noel. He kisses her forehead. "Sweet dreams," he whispers, before turning to leave.

Chapter 12

Eddie opens the apartment door to find Lincoln half into a bottle of Eagle Rare. He looks worse for the wear. "I don't think that stuff works on you like it does on me, bud."

Lincoln doesn't laugh, but appreciates Eddie's attempt at humor. "I knew her—Sara. She's dead and it's my fault. Soon that little girl and Beth will be dead, too." Lincoln grimaces as he solemnly takes another drink of the bourbon.

"I'm not gonna let that happen, Lincoln." Eddie takes the bottle from the table. "I need to shower and get back to Beth's to make sure that nothing happens to those two. Are you gonna be okay here?"

Lincoln shoes Eddie away. "Of course."

"Hey, man. Why can't you just freeze them like you did me? Then I just go find them and rip out their hearts and stuff."

"I already told you. It doesn't work like that. I didn't write that into their story like I did yours. I can't affect them in any way that wasn't written into their original story. I'm powerless against them, hence the need for you," Lincoln slurs back as he slams a fist against the table.

"Lucky me."

"Don't be ungrateful, you prick. I gave you everything and everyone…"

"Yeah and you can take it away. I get it."

"You better get it. And you better get the four remaining vampires before they get anyone else. There's the two females you saw, Lisa and Courtney, another female Jennifer, and a wise-ass male named Perry. He's their leader. Kill them all by tomorrow night."

"Whatever, man. I'm getting a shower. See if you can write the female vamps in there so I can *take care of* them." Eddie slams the bathroom door hard enough to shake the barren walls.

"It doesn't… work… like…" Lincoln mumbles before he passes out at the table.

Chapter 13

The walk back to Beth's apartment is eerily quiet. Usually there are people out and about on the streets, but tonight it's just Eddie and the wind.

Eddie uses Beth's spare key to open the outer security door to the apartment building and quickly climbs the stairs to her floor. As he starts down the corridor towards Beth's door, Eddie notices an extremely attractive woman loitering in the hallway. The closer he gets, the more beautiful she gets. Her brown hair shapes her face nicely, her eyes sparkle brighter than any star, and when she beams at him, he feels his heart flutter.

"Lookin' to have some fun tonight, honey?" She bites her lower lip and grins.

Eddie smiles back, but turns to put the key in Beth's door. "I think I'm all *funned* out for tonight, but I appreciate the offer."

"You're cute. You sure you don't want to invite me in?" She adjusts her shirt so Eddie can get a better look at her perky breasts.

Eddie swallows hard. "Yeah. Don't think I'd be much fun tonight, anyway." He steps inside and begins to close the door.

"Wait! Take my card, sweetie." The woman holds out a pink business card which Eddie reaches out of the door and grabs. She winks and walks away, which gives Eddie a chance to admire her shapely backside. She adds a little extra hip swing to her walk before she turns her head and beams back at him. "Maybe we can grab a coffee soon."

Chapter 14

Eddie closes the door and leans against it as he scans the woman's card. His attraction to her is obviously physical, but she also had a mysterious aura about her that is drawing him to her.

Jennifer Green – Your Escort to Ecstasy.

Huh? Where...? What are you reading? Lincoln's startled voice pops into Eddie's head.

Ah, Lincoln. I see you're back amongst the living.

Not really. I forgot what this stuff does to me. How do you do it?

Really? The whole you-made-me-an-alcoholic-superhero thing doesn't ring a bell?

Antihero, actually. Where did you get that card?

Super-hot chick outside Beth's apartment. Like, two minutes ago. I take it you were still in a bourbon coma for that conversation?

Eddie, that's Jennifer. THE Jennifer. Vampire Jennifer. You need to drink as much bourbon as you can and go after her.

The Editor

Come on, man. I'm freakin' tired, and I don't think Beth has any more bourbon here.

Cupboard above the fridge. Glasses are in the cabinet just to the left of the sink.

How would you...? Eddie starts as he opens the cupboards to find things exactly as Lincoln had said.

Just drink up and call the number on that card.

Ah, Yes, Massa, Eddie replies sarcastically. *Next time I open this cupboard, I hope you "know" that there will be some Blanton's or Eagle Rare in it. This stuff is shitty.*

Beth's favorite. Lincoln smirks smugly, thinking that at least Eddie and Beth won't have their favorite bourbon in common.

We still both love other things. Eddie grins, remembering their time together the previous night. *Yeah, that hearing thoughts shit goes both ways, buddy. Anyways, bottoms up. I got me a vampire hottie to slay. Get your ass over to Beth's so that when she wakes up she doesn't think I bailed on her.*

Chapter 15

Eddie can feel a wave of nervous excitement rush over him as he dials the number on the card.

"Hello?" the sultry voice on the other end of the line answers.

"Um, hey. Jennifer?"

"Yes. Who's this?"

"Um... it's, uh... Ed... the guy you just gave your card to in the hallway."

"The little fat one or the tall sexy one?"

Eddie blushes at being called sexy. "Well, I'm not little or fat so, I guess..."

"Oh, don't guess, sweetie. You're as sexy as they come. Did you have a change of heart? I'm just outside the building. I can come back up and we can have the time of our lives."

DO NOT let her into the apartment with Beth and Noel inside! Lincoln's voice rings loud in Eddie's head.

No shit, Sherlock.

"Well, I was thinking maybe I'd take you up on that coffee offer first. Then we can see where things lead."

"That sounds even better. I like me a caffeinated man. Only problem is that I don't know many places that are open for coffee right now."

"I know a place. Just give me a second to call a cab and I'll be right down."

"That's cute. A cab." Jennifer laughs. "I'll get us there."

Eddie hangs up the phone and makes sure that all of his weapons are hidden inside his coat.

Chapter 16

Eddie makes his way outside into the wet, dark night. A black Cadillac CT6 with windows as dark as the paint is parked across the street. The driver's side window lowers, revealing the face of a large man. Eddie cautiously walks toward the car.

"Miss Jenny requests your presents." The driver's voice lacks even the slightest hint of emotion. A rear window slides down and the woman from the hallway winks at Eddie.

"What's with Jersey Shore, here?" Eddie grins and nods toward the driver.

"*Presence*, Rocko. Presence. No 'T'. We've been over this," Jennifer opens the back door and slides over to make room for Eddie.

"Sorry, Miss Jenny. Where to?"

"That's up to this handsome fella." Jennifer slides closer and takes a hold of Eddie's right hand.

"Jim Jim's. It's in the strip district."

"Take the long way, Rocko." Jennifer presses the button to close the window between Rocko and them as she moves to straddle Eddie. Before he can protest, her lips are against his and every one of Eddie's senses explodes. Jennifer must feel it too, because she momentarily loses her breath before going right back at it.

Eddie feels as though he's staring into the sun, while eating a burning ice cube, while a train whistle sounds non-stop in his ear, all while inside a bag of flower potpourri. The only thing is, instead of it being painful, it's sheer bliss.

Lincoln, how do I stop this?

He gets no reply.

Eddie has no idea how long they've been in the car, he only knows that it was not long enough. When the vehicle comes to a stop, Jennifer reluctantly climbs off of him and opens the door closest to the curb.

"This is the place?" She raises her left eyebrow as she looks out at an unimpressive diner.

"You said you wanted coffee. They have the strongest around. At least, they do at three a.m."

She laughs. "I'll try anything thrice."

"I bet you would." Eddie smirks as he places his hand on the small of her back and guides her into the diner.

They sit down at a sticky table and a waitress plops two less-than-sanitary-looking menus down in front of them.

"Thanks, Berta." Eddie smiles, getting a weird *How'd you know my name?* look from the waitress.

That's my memory, Eddie. Be careful. Just because you know someone doesn't mean they know you.

Oh, now you're talking to me.

What's that supposed to mean?

Earlier in the car. She kissed me and I felt like each organ in my body was having its own miniature orgasm.

You kissed her?

Did you listen to anything I said? She kissed me—then I kissed her. A lot. But don't worry about this. I got it.

You damn well better, Eddie.

"You okay, sweetie?" Jennifer looks genuinely concerned. "You seem to be really thinking about something. We don't have to do anything besides get coffee." She offers with a smile that Eddie still finds seductive.

"Um, yeah, I'm fine. I just can't decide what kind of omelet I want," Eddie replies feigning interest in the menu.

"Just no onions, okay?" She again flashes her seductive smile.

"And no decaf coffee, right?" Eddie's tone is cold.

The vampire laughs nervously. "Um, right. I want you to stay up with me tonight."

They make small talk as Eddie tries to remain distant until the food gets to the table.

"Finally." She fidgets in her chair uncomfortably before taking a big whiff of her food.

"You aren't one of those girls that just smells their food and doesn't eat it, are you?" Eddie teases.

"Hardly. I just need to get the stench of that ivory you have hidden in your coat out of my nose." She grins again, but this time it's more wicked than seductive.

Eddie's stomach drops.

"Relax, sweetie. We aren't going to hurt each other." Her smile softens a bit.

"Oh no? What makes you so sure about that?" Eddie leans back in his chair, eyebrows raised.

"You didn't feel that in the car? That type of stuff only happens in books."

Eddie bursts into laughter at the irony of the statement.

"We're meant to be, Eddie. Soulmates, or whatever. I'm ninety-nine percent sure that you killed two of my closest friends, and I'm one hundred percent ready to forgive you for it *and* to trust you with my life. In all my years of existence, I have never felt anything like that. I'll do anything for you, and trust me, I know how crazy-stupid this all sounds."

Eddie nods, but can't deny that he feels sort of the same way. "Yeah. You sound certifiable. Just out of curiosity, though, exactly how many years of existence do you think you've had?"

"I'm just under half a millennium old. I was a lady in waiting for Mary Queen of Scots until Perry, my vampire father, showed up in court."

"Vampire father? You mean maker?" Eddie laughs.

"No." Jennifer answers sternly. "We were still made by God, with the help of our parents, of course. Maker is a stupid term that some horror author thought sounded cute. And while we're at it, we don't have an uncontrollable lust for our vampire fathers or feel anything but what you would feel for your father. We're not sex fiends who just sleep with anyone or anything, either. Well, Matt is—or was— but not all of us are, anyway. We can go to church and take communion; most of us are extremely religious, in fact. Sunlight doesn't burn us, and we don't sparkle in it either. Upon first glance, nothing sets us apart from humans except that we're extremely attractive, of course." She winks.

"So, you don't just sleep with anybody, huh? Just the good paying guys?" The words escape Eddie's mouth before he has time to think them through.

"What is *that* supposed to mean?" The vampire

shrinks back in her chair and lowers her eyes, seeming genuinely hurt.

Eddie's stomach drops again after seeing the pain in her eyes.

"It's just... your card says you're going to *Escort* me to *Ecstasy*." Eddies blushes, trying to laugh it off.

"Ummm, yeah. I show my clients all the area's hot spots. We have a blast. Anything they desire... except sex with me."

"Right. Then why'd you ask to come up to the apartment when I called you?"

"Oh, that was because I needed you to invite me in so that I could go in and kill the woman and kid later." She takes a bite of breakfast potatoes.

Eddie stares at her, slack-jawed.

"What? I'm not gonna do it now. I *couldn't* do anything to hurt you, even if I wanted to."

Somehow Eddie knows that he could never hurt Jennifer either.

"So, what do we do now?" He picks at his omelet, waiting for a response.

"Hopefully we kiss some more." She blushes. "Then I guess I need to work on a way to better control my... urges."

"You can't live without blood," Eddie whispers.

"Doesn't mean I have to kill. Maybe I could find a willing donor." She lifts her beautiful pale blue eyes to meet his gaze.

Eddie laughs. "Who, me?"

"It can actually be quite pleasant. Enjoyable even." Color floods her cheeks as she stares back down at her food.

Eddie finishes his omelet and motions for Berta to bring the check. "We can figure all of this out later. There's someone we need to talk to first. Maybe he can help us understand all of this better. You ready?" He pushes his chair back from the table and gets to his feet.

Suddenly Jennifer is at his side with her hand in his. Even the holding of hands sends shock waves all through his system. "Where to next, honey?"

Chapter 17

Rocko takes the long way back to Beth's apartment, allowing Eddie and Jennifer to experiment some more with their new-found infatuation. The streets are fairly empty, save for a few police cars and an ambulance that whizzes by them at one point. Eddie and Jennifer don't notice; they're together in a far-off utopia.

Finally, Rocko rolls to a slow stop in front of the apartment. "Will I be coming in, Miss Jenny?"

Jennifer looks at Eddie then shakes her head. "No, I'll be fine. You can head home, Rocko. Thank you."

"Is he—" Eddie nods back toward the car.

"Like me? No. I just compelled him to be my loyal employee." She notices Eddie's brow furrow and continues. "He was a homeless alcoholic. Now he is a very well-paid chauffeur who has no vices." She straightens her back and holds her head high.

Eddie's face softens and he takes Jennifer by the hand and heads into the building.

Lincoln, I'm home. Jennifer is with me. It's okay, though. Something has happened.

What?! Don't you dare bring her up here.

Too late. Just open the door.

Lincoln opens the door slowly and Eddie casually strolls in. Jennifer lingers in the doorway as Lincoln stares at her ghost-faced. Beth is on the couch. She smiles weakly at Eddie and he nervously waves back.

"Come on in, Jennifer. We've got a lot to explain to both of them." Eddie motions for her to follow him into the apartment.

Jennifer attempts to enter, but bounces back as if repelled by the doorway.

Lincoln's scowl turns into a smile and he begins to laugh. "Oh, that's right! You can't. And you thought this was *his* house? He doesn't have a house."

"Lincoln, what's wrong with you? Sweetie, you can come in." Beth smiles kindly.

"No—" Lincoln starts, but Jennifer has a hand around his throat before he can say any more.

"Put him down, love." Eddie chuckles.

Jennifer releases her hold on Lincoln and goes to a chair across the room and sits, arms folded.

"Love?" Beth asks, a lump forming in her throat and tears welling up in her eyes.

The Editor

Eddie's cheeks burn. He goes to the cupboard and pours himself a large glass of the cheap bourbon.

Lincoln runs his hands through his hair. *Shit. How can I make Beth understand all of this?*

You're the author. Start telling the story, Eddie eyes Lincoln as he drops a few ice cubes into his glass.

Lincoln sits back down next to Beth and takes her hand. "Beth, what I am about to tell you will sound completely irrational. I'm not crazy, and I can prove it all to you if you'll just allow me to."

Beth scans each person's face with confusion on her own. Eddie has his eyes closed, grimacing at the taste of the bourbon. Jennifer has moved to the edge of her seat and is biting her lower lip, and Lincoln grimaces as if he is trying to pass a kidney stone the size of a golf ball.

"Something happened. I don't fully understand how it happened, only that it did. Some of my worst characters are now... alive."

Beth stares at him like he has four heads.

Lincoln clears his throat and continues. "You remember last year when I was really struggling and I did that parody *Vriends?*"

"The vampires who only drink caffeinated blood?" She scrunches her nose and scratches her head. Jennifer's head snaps in her direction.

"Yes. *That,*" he motions to the gorgeous brunette in the chair, "is Jennifer." She flashes a fanged smile, as if on cue.

Beth jumps back in horror. "Did she kill...?"

"No!" Eddie shakes his head. "Those two are dead. Jennifer is different." He casts an admiring look at the vampire who returns his look with a lustful smile.

"Eddie, get it together," Lincoln snaps. "How is she different?"

"Easy." Jennifer's voice is calm. "We imprinted." She shrugs.

"Imprinted? I thought that was a werewolf thing?" Beth looks at Lincoln before rolling her eyes.

Lincoln buries his face in his hands. "I may have *borrowed* the idea." He sounds truly ashamed. "Like I said, I was struggling."

You may be a hack, but I'm not complaining. Imprinting is some good shit. Eddie nods in Lincoln's direction and subtly raises his glass.

"None of this makes any sense, Lincoln. If your creations really did come to life, you should be able to destroy them, right? This is just some psycho who actually liked *Vriends*. And by the way Eddie, SCREW YOU!" Beth yells as she hurls a coffee cup at Eddie.

Jennifer catches the cup before a drop can spill. She licks her lips slowly before finishing it in one gulp.

"Next best thing to caffeinated blood." She smirks.

Lincoln sighs as he gets ready to explain his dilemma again. "*Vriends* is completed. I can't make any changes to their story. They have free will now, but I can prove that what I'm saying is true." He punches a few keys on his laptop. Suddenly, they hear a high-pitched bark and a furry brown and black puppy that resembles a gremlin as much as it does a dog, walks out from behind the couch. "Meet Eddie's dog."

"Mr. Eko!" Eddie grins from ear-to-ear as the puppy jumps into his arms and licks him on the lips.

Beth's face goes whiter than Jennifer's. Jennifer scrunches her face, also seemingly disturbed, more so by the lip licking than by the puppy itself.

"A puppy!" Noel screams in excitement as she enters the room. Beth quickly stands between her and Jennifer as if she could actually protect her.

"Jennifer is no danger to you or Noel now. She couldn't hurt you even if she wanted to, as long as it would also hurt Eddie. Side effect of imprinting," Lincoln explains, almost in disbelief himself. "Eddie also had no choice but to fall in love with her, if that makes you feel any better."

"It doesn't. Noel, why don't you take Mr. Eko into my room and try to get some more sleep? Okay, sweetie?" Beth guides her niece back into the bedroom.

"So, I'm not real?" Jennifer's voice quivers.

"You—*we*— are very real. Just... new to this particular world," Eddie attempts to explain but stops, realizing that he doesn't understand it himself.

"None of this is relevant right now," Lincoln snaps. "All that matters is how we're going to kill Perry, Courtney, Lisa and any other monsters that I may have inadvertently created. Any ideas?"

Chapter 18

"Why don't I just talk to them? Get them to stop killing," Jennifer maintains eye contact with Lincoln as she calmly sets the cup down on the coffee table. "Courtney has more fun seducing her prey than killing it, and she gets attached to certain ones and lets them live anyway. Lisa will do whatever Courtney does, so it should be easy."

Lincoln closes his eyes, considers his characters, and shakes his head. "Even if that works, and they stop killing, if anyone finds out that there are vampires in Pittsburgh... plus, Perry will never stop killing. *He* is a monster."

Jennifer bares her fangs. "*He* is my *father!* And *he* is the way he is because of you, so you can find a way to stop him *without* killing him."

Eddie puts a comforting hand on Jennifer's shoulder and looks at Lincoln.

I'm not going to be able to kill this guy if he means this much to her.

I know, I know. We'll just have to see how everything plays out. At least she won't allow Perry to hurt any of us while we figure everything out.

Lincoln stands and walks over to Beth's living room window. He watches the early morning traffic for a minute while he strokes his beard.

"Okay, Jennifer. Talk to them, but this is a zero-tolerance type situation. Make it clear... No more killing. *None.*"

The vampire nods and gets to her feet. Eddie follows her as she moves toward the door. She turns and grabs him by the stubble on his face and presses her lips into his. "You can't meet them just yet, sweetie. Let me talk to them first. If all goes well, maybe we can have coff—lunch tomorrow. All of us." She gestures at the room.

Before Eddie can protest, Jennifer is gone. Eddie looks to Beth, whose mouth hangs open, and then to Lincoln, who hasn't moved from the window. "What do we do now?"

Lincoln doesn't break his empty stare. "We wait."

Chapter 19

*October 29*th
Renaissance Hotel Pittsburgh's Cultural District

Jennifer lies awake on the bed in her luxuriously appointed suite on the concierge level of the hotel. Hotels are the housing loophole for vampires. A human doesn't have to invite them in since any paying customer is typically welcome. It's also usually a good place to feed since they can enter any room; the occupants don't own them. This hotel has a total of four concierge suites, and the vampires currently occupy all of them. Perry has the largest suite, Jennifer has her own, Courtney and Lisa share one, and the final suite was David and Matt's, but is now unoccupied.

Theoretically, Courtney or Lisa could move into the unoccupied suite, but knowing them, Jennifer finds that unlikely. Those two are as close as two mated vampires can be without imprinting.

Jennifer's private concierge, Samantha, just stopped by to make sure that the mini bar was stocked and unwittingly satisfied Jennifer's true hunger. Jennifer has a fondness for Samantha, though; she would never drain the young woman beyond repair. She just erases her memory of the feeding and sends her on her way with a large tip and an even larger smile.

Jennifer tried the other girls' suite before heading to her own, but was stopped at the door by their concierge, who politely explained that they required "complete privacy." She decided not to push it. Her talk with them could wait, so she left the young man to his daydreams about what was happening inside.

Her stomach is now in a knot as she looks into her own pale blue eyes in the bathroom mirror. What is she going to say to Perry to convince him that he has to stop killing in order for their brood to live in peace? Her father truly is a monster who says he kills his victims because he likes the taste of fear mixed with their caffeinated blood. "You can't get that taste without death," he always says.

Jennifer applies another layer of bright red lipstick and some of her patented vanilla perfume and heads to her father's suite. There is no telling what kind of company he may have, but he'll certainly have company, since he can't stand to be alone. As she approaches the suite, her father's concierge Brandon nods and tells her to go ahead in, the door is open.

"Quite a party tonight." He smiles, but it can't mask the worry all over his face.

Jennifer returns his smile and quickly ducks into the suite. The scene that unfolds before her eyes is a mix between a slasher film and late-night Cinemax. As she scans the room for Perry, a nude man stumbles into her and mumbles something about giving her anything she wants. She notices his wedding ring and stares into his glassy brown eyes.

"Go home to your wife. If you came here on your own, buy her something nice and never stop making this up to her. If you were compelled to come here, just forget this night ever happened." The man starts to leave the suite, but she calls back to him, remembering how literally humans take being compelled. "Put some clothes on first, sir."

She finally locates her father sitting on a chair in the corner with a young couple on his lap.

"For real, Dad? Could you be any more cliché?"

"Ah. Jenny! Try some of these two. She had the pumpkin spice latte and he had something with cinnamon. If you mix them together, it tastes like fall." Perry laughs.

"I just ate, but thanks," Jennifer replies politely.

"Are you sure? It's to die for," Perry winks before baring his fangs and tearing the man's throat out. The young woman looks horrified but is unable to scream.

Jennifer knows that her father likes it this way. He compels them to remain silent and motionless, but allows them to feel the fear that makes them taste so delicious. Once the woman gets to her maximum level of fear, he bites into her femoral artery and drains her as well.

Jennifer looks around the room. Dozens of bodies are scattered about, some barely clinging to life, some long dead, and a few— the Cinemax crew— are doing their thing without a care in the world. They'll be snacks sooner rather than later, but for now, they're serving as her father's live entertainment.

"Looks like you've had quite a satisfying night, Dad."

Perry scoffs as he watches a few coeds go at it. "You know this is just another weekend, sweetie. If you aren't hungry, why did you come over? There is a college guy over there that I swear is part horse." He winks and grins.

"Eeew, Dad, come on! I just need to talk to you about all this... killing." The knot in her stomach tightens.

"For the love of God! This again? We are vampires. We kill. This," he motions toward the coeds, "is our food."

"Dad, you know we can feed without killing them. At this rate, you're going to eat the whole damn city in a week. *Then* what are you doing to do?" She puts her hands on her hips, beginning to mount her normal argument.

"We'll move to Cleveland." The voice is not her father's and she whirls around and is met with the smiling, blood-covered face of an unfamiliar young vampire.

She spins back to face her father. "Who...THE...F—"

"Jenny, Buffy. Buffy, Jenny." He gets to his feet as he makes the uncomfortable introduction. "Meet your mother-sister."

"I can't believe you! You swore you'd never," Jennifer starts, as tears well up in her eyes. "Buffy? Are you *shitting* me?"

"That was before some asshole killed my sons! And I'm tired of sleeping with mortals. I need more. I need... an eternal love!" Perry's outburst causes even the Cinemax crew to pause for a second. He closes his eyes and takes a moment to regain his composure. "Don't I deserve it?" This time the words come out more softly, but he gets no reply besides Buffy moving to his side. "Anyway, I saw Buffy at the strip club doing an extremely ironic vampire slayer routine and knew it was our destiny to be together. So yes. I made another. And together we will satisfy every urge that we have from now until the end of time. If God wants to stop us, He will, but I haven't seen any signs that point that way." He cups Buffy's face between his hands and plants a deep and passionate kiss on his vampire bride's lips.

Jennifer's eyes shift down to her feet. "I imprinted on a slayer." The words would have been inaudible to human ears.

Perry abruptly stops his kiss with Buffy. "Slayer... the band? Which one?" He raises an eyebrow.

"No, Dad. A vampire slayer. But listen, it could be a good—"

Perry glares coldly at Jennifer as she speaks. He knows that she could not—and would not—lie about something so serious.

Before she even knows what has happened, Perry is holding the amulet that he had given her the day he turned her; one that had not left her neck since that day. Her eyes grow wide as she stares at the stone dangling from his hand. "Dad, what're you—"

"Your brood connection is severed. Leave us immediately." The dead look in Perry's eyes confirms that any fondness that he may have once had for her is now gone. His eyes betray no emotion. No sadness, no pain, not even any anger. How could he feel nothing after all this time together?

Jennifer's heart shatters. She knows that he knows she had no choice in this matter, and the fact that he shows no understanding or compassion is devastating.

"What does that mean?" Buffy looks at Perry with the curious eyes of a child.

"We're at war." Jennifer spits backs before reaching into the young vampire's chest cavity and pulling out her heart with one hand while spinning and separating her head from her body with the other. Before her father can react, she's at the bottom floor of the hotel and in to Rocco's car which, thankfully, she had summoned as a precaution.

"Where to, Miss Jenny?"

Chapter 20

Eddie springs to his feet when he hears the knock at the door. He's prepared for anyone and anything; he's been sipping bourbon since the moment Jennifer left to meet her family.

"She's alone," Lincoln says from his seat by the window.

Beth opens the door, allowing the forlorn vampire to enter.

"Jennifer, what's wrong?" Eddie pulls her into a tight embrace. He can smell the blood on her before he sees it and knows that things did not go as she had hoped. He squeezes her tighter and then guides her to Beth's couch. She sits between Beth and Eddie. Lincoln makes his way closer to join the conversation as well.

"He... he broke our bond," she sobs. "He made a vampire bride, which is gross, and he chose killing with her over... over me."

Everyone sits quietly and allows Jennifer a few minutes to grieve until Lincoln finally breaks the silence.

"Courtney and Lisa?"

"I didn't get to talk to them before he broke our bond. They were... together at the time, but now they'll be on opposite sides of this."

"Of course." Lincoln nods. "You sired Courtney, and Perry sired Lisa. Courtney is in real trouble if she's still there with them. Three vampires versus one is not good odds."

"It would've just been her and Lisa, and Lisa's love for her would have allowed Courtney time to escape." Jennifer sniffles. "What do you care anyway? You want us all dead, remember? That's why you made Eddie."

Lincoln winces. "I created Eddie to correct my mistakes. So far, he has fixed three of them... He's only killed two. Maybe we can find other ways to resolve our differences with those that are willing to try."

"Well, we're gonna have to kill Perry. No way around that." Jennifer holds her head in her hands.

Lincoln paces back and forth behind the couch. "What about Perry and his new vampire?" he asks, still shocked that Perry would create another. In the story, Perry vowed to never create another vampire after an attempt to create a seventh member of the brood, Gunther, went terribly wrong.

"I killed the bitch on my way out. The way he looked... he was stunned. He's going to kill me— slowly."

Jennifer buries her head in Eddie's chiseled chest.

Eddie looks at Lincoln. *I can destroy this guy easily, right?*

Well, yes. You can defeat him— and will— but what kind of story would it be if I made it easy for you to defeat everyone?

Hey, asshole. In case you missed it, this isn't a story anymore. These freaks are killing real people. Real people that YOU know.

Lincoln grimaces, and the pain on his face is enough to make Eddie feel bad that he went there, but it needed to be said.

"Jennifer, I'll never let your father, or anyone else for that matter, hurt you, my love." Eddie squeezes the vampire tighter against his chest.

"He's not my father anymore."

Chapter 21

A second knock on the door draws everyone's attention, but no one moves to answer it this time. Eddie reaches for an ivory stake inside his coat on a nearby chair.

"I'll get it!" Noel says as she sprints to the front door with Mr. Eko close behind.

The door is open before Beth can shriek "No!" and standing in front of the little girl is a thin woman with short black hair that flares out at the shoulders. She wears a short skirt and a tight shirt that accentuates all the right places. Eddie recognizes her as one of the college girls from the coffee shop.

The woman's sly smile quickly turns to a snarl when she sees Noel, who jumps back in terror. Mr. Eko sinks his teeth into the woman's two-thousand-dollar thigh-high Jimmy Choo's, but she doesn't even flinch. Her gaze is set on Noel.

"Little girl. Invite me in."

Before Noel can speak, Jennifer stands in front of her, breaking the link between vampire and child. "That won't be necessary, dear. You can come in as soon as you calm down and swear an oath to your mother that you no longer have any desire to hurt anyone in this room or to kill any innocent human being ever again."

"Mom! That's not fair!" The *younger* vampire shouts. "Why are you protecting them? *HE* killed Matt and David. *SHE...*" Courtney points an angry finger at Noel. "*...and I assume now *all of them*, know about us. And what happened between you and Perry? Why do I want to kill my girlfriend?"

Oh? Hot lesbian vampires? Really, Lincoln?

Shut up, Eddie.

Jennifer looks at her daughter across the doorway with love. "Because, dear, I imprinted on *HIM*. And he has a fondness for all of *THEM*."

"Oh." She pauses, clearly caught off guard. "Well, okay, momma. I swear to never harm any of the people in this apartment and to protect them with my life." She smiles honestly.

"And..."

The young vampire bites her lower lip. "...And never to kill anyone who doesn't deserve it."

Jennifer looks to Beth. "Invite my daughter in." Beth hesitates and looks at Lincoln.

He nods. "She swore an oath to her sire. Any failure to comply will result in a type of... involuntary suicide."

The Editor

Eddie scoops Noel up in his arms and carries her toward the kitchen, away from Courtney. Mr. Eko finally lets go of Courtney's boot and follows them to the other side of the room.

Beth looks back at the vampire in her doorway. "Umm... okay then. Come on in."

Chapter 22

Courtney strolls into the room, back straight and head held high, with an heir of superiority. Her eyes scan each person without interest until she sees Beth. Her already slow beating, vampiric heart skips a beat. The carnal attraction is instantaneous, but this is nothing out of the ordinary for Courtney. Lisa was the only thing keeping her from being a full-on womanizer. "Hello." She flashes her most seductive smile and holds out a dainty hand.

"Umm, hi." Beth quickly looks away after awkwardly shaking Courtney's hand.

"Okay." Jennifer promptly directs Courtney to a seat between her and Eddie on the couch. "We have a war to plan. First, we need to elect a leader and all vow to follow him or her, no matter what. We get through this together or not at all."

"Well, how about Eddie?" Beth calls back as she guides Noel and Mr. Eko back into the bedroom where there is a television to distract them.

The Editor

Everyone seems to agree that Eddie would be a good choice, but Eddie has another thought.

"Thank you all, but I'm a soldier. There is one person who has an intimate knowledge of our enemies and that person is Lincoln. I'm a man of action, but being a leader sometimes requires a lack of action. It requires thought, planning. I'm not sure that I like Lincoln, but I do trust that he'll do what is best for everyone involved. So, I nominate Lincoln as our leader."

Thank you, Eddie.

Jennifer stares at the ceiling for a moment. "It makes sense. The rest of us have strong attachments to some in the group that could potentially leave others in jeopardy. Lincoln is attached to all of us in some way, but not overly attached to any one of us."

Eddie notices Lincoln glance down at the ground momentarily.

Except maybe Beth, huh, Lincoln?

Lincoln doesn't respond. He just stares Eddie directly in the eyes.

Eddie stares back until Lincoln finally blinks. *Just don't get the rest of us killed.*

Chapter 23

Lincoln, somewhat hesitantly, stands and walks back toward the windows so that everyone can see him. He has never been comfortable being a leader in the past, but he knows that this, however unfair it may be, is his mess to clean up.

"Okay, so what do we know?"

"There are two of them and three of us," Eddie's voice is full of bravado. "Let's end this quickly."

Courtney scoffs and Jennifer laughs like Eddie is an innocent child who has just said something adorable. "Oh, sweetie. Perry had already made another. Now we're at war. He will make as many soldiers as he can until his enemies cease to exist."

"And Lisa can't stand to be alone. She'll make Perry a mate in exchange for one of her own." Courtney's voice shakes as tears begin to form in her eyes.

"Assuming he doesn't want to mate with his own progeny again." Jennifer spits back in disgust.

"But wouldn't Lisa's progeny be like his... grandchild?" Beth wrinkles her nose.

Jennifer just rolls her eyes and shakes her head, but Courtney grins. "No, sweetie. The bond does not span generations."

Lincoln clears his throat to regain control of the conversation. "Okay, so we're facing an unknown number of enemies, most of which will have unknown powers. We know Perry and Lisa's powers and therefore know their weaknesses."

"What do you mean unknown powers?" Eddie asks.

"Every vampire has a unique... gift. They allow us to protect ourselves from our enemies. If you master your unique gift, you live a long life," Jennifer explains kindly. "Take me for instance. Besides my killer ass, I'm unnaturally fast."

"All vampires are unnaturally fast, my love."

"No, Eddie. I couldn't hit her if I wanted to," Courtney explains.

"Yes, and it allowed me to kill his bimbo and escape while he stood there and watched." Jennifer leans back on the couch and props her feet up on Beth's coffee table, knocking a magazine on the floor.

"And what's your *power*, Courtney." Beth turns to the vampire, sincerely interested.

"Lust, baby doll, lust. I can make any vampire want me, at least long enough that they hesitate to kill me," she replies in her bubbly voice as she picks up the magazine.

Beth looks uncomfortably at Lincoln, who shakes his head in self-disgust and goes on. "Perry can teleport and Lisa can freeze things with her touch."

Beth nods and Eddie's eyes perk up.

"Ah, so that's why the jock turned to stone before I killed him."

Courtney gawks at Eddie. "You killed him *after* he turned to stone?"

"How in the world are we supposed to beat them if they create an endless army of superhero vampires?" Beth shouts as she smacks Lincoln on the arm.

Lincoln winces, more at her anger than at the pain of the actual slap. "First, *you* are not to defeat anyone. Second, they are super-villains, not super heroes. And third, Eddie's superpower is that he can adapt whatever power he needs to defeat his closest enemy."

"As long as I have my bourbon—which we're dangerously low on." Eddie holds up the bottle. Before he knows it, three bottles of Eagle Rare are on the table in front of him and Jennifer has her lips against his.

"Thanks, love." Is all he can manage after he regains his composure.

Jennifer hands Lincoln a small strip of paper. "You owe me one hundred eleven dollars and eighty-six cents." She smirks at Eddie as she sits back down next to him.

Lincoln looks at the receipt. "You should've gone to Wine and Spirits, it's cheap... Never mind."

Beth shakes her head in disgust. "So, Eddie is the superhero?"

"More an antihero, but yes." Lincoln smiles kindly. "We need to strike soon before they have time to build an army. Where will they be most likely to recruit their prey?"

"Strip club," both vampires answer in unison.

"Good, then that's where we plan to attack," Lincoln says.

Beth leans forward in her seat. "Which club? I know—"

Lincoln quickly cuts her off. "Beth, this is too dangerous for you. You're all Noel has now. You need to think about keeping her safe and let us avenge Sara."

Beth knows that Lincoln is right, but she can't help but feel useless. "Then how *can* I help?"

Lincoln places a comforting hand on her shoulder. "First, you can plan Sara's memorial. Other than that, just don't let that little girl out of your sight. We'll keep you informed on everything that happens. I promise."

Chapter 24

Lincoln formulates a plan: Eddie will enter the club alone. Jennifer and Courtney will watch the outside from the diner across the street as backup.

Eddie enters the dark, smoky club, walks to the bar, and orders a bourbon on the rocks. He scans the room. Seeing no immediate threat, he lets his eyes linger on the stage for a few moments.

There's no one here, man. Why don't I try the hotel?

He can teleport wherever he wants. Find the back room, it's more secluded.

How do you...? Never mind.

Eddie sips his bourbon and looks toward a curtain in the back corner of the club. A beautiful young woman with skin the color of the caramel macchiato he ordered a few days back approaches him with a wide smile on her face.

"You wanna head back there, sugar? We can have all kinds of fun."

"I'm not sure it's fun that I'm looking for," he replies softly.

The Editor

"Well, it's forty for the normal stuff, but any of that kinky shit is gonna cost you extra, sugar." She grabs his hand and pulls him towards the curtain.

As they wait for a couple in front of them to have their credit card processed, Eddie's curiosity gets the best of him. "So why do you do this? Don't tell me you're paying for med school or law school, either."

Caramel flashes her wide smile again. "Oh no, sugar. I do this because I love it. Look at me. When a man looks at me with desire in his eyes, I know at that moment I have this... power over him. I just crave that power. I don't do anything I don't want to, and I make a ton of money. It's a win-win, darlin'."

Eddie hands the bouncer his forty-dollar entry fee and follows Caramel into the room. It's lit with an eerie, red light bulb. She pushes Eddie down onto a couch and begins to dance seductively in front of him.

Eddie scans the room. A tall blonde woman and a muscular man on the adjacent couch both have their mouths on the neck of a busty raven-haired woman. Caramel continues to dance, but Eddie is growing uncomfortable. The couple's lips never leave the stripper's skin and her body begins to go limp. Just as Caramel begins to remove her top Eddie springs to his feet and approaches the other group.

"What the fu..." Caramel shouts as Eddie brushes her aside.

"Let her go," Eddie growls as he glares down at the trio. The man and woman slowly pull their faces away from the stripper's neck. Blood covers both of their mouths and floods down their victim's neck and into her ample cleavage.

"Oh, now that's some messed up shit." Caramel scrambles back towards the curtain.

"Get out of here!" Eddie waves her out of the room as he pulls an ivory stake from his jacket. Both vampires recoil instinctively, but the female still has her hand on the stripper and the young woman's body instantly turns to ice.

"Now look what you've done," the female snarls. "I don't like frozen food!" She swipes at the frozen stripper, smashing her into thousands of pieces. With a flick of her wrist, the male springs to his feet, ready to attack Eddie, but Eddie hurls the stake directly at his heart. Much to Eddie's surprise, the stake bounces off the man who seems to have developed a metal-like armor over his entire body. The male vampire swipes at Eddie, catching him off guard and knocking him back against a wall.

Ugh! A little help here, Lincoln!
Just trust your gift, Eddie.

"What's a matter, slayer? You never saw an inde-structible vampire before?" The female mocks as she relaxes on the couch, apparently enjoying the show. The male approaches Eddie slowly, allowing him time to get back to his feet. Eddie dodges a jab and catches the vampire's arm when he throws a right hook. He bends the vampire's arm backwards and sweeps his left foot, knocking him on his back.

Eddie glances down at his right hand, which is glowing a bright shade of orange—the color of molten steel. Suddenly he knows what to do. He drives his hand into the vampire's chest and his fist melts the armor. He wraps his hand around the vampire's heart and squeezes. The vampire's eyes grow wide as he begins to gasp for air and feebly claw at Eddie's arms.

Eddie snaps his hand back, tearing the heart from the vampire's chest and throwing it across the room. His left hand has morphed into a bright orange knife-like blade. Eddie brings it violently down across the vampire's neck. The blow is so fierce that the man's head rolls to the feet of the woman on the couch, who stares at Eddie in disbelief.

Eddie grins at the woman as his hands return to their normal state. "Lisa, I presume?"

The woman stammers as she scampers back-ward against the wall. Eddie picks up the ivory stake and takes a step toward her. He grins and drives the stake forward but just as it's about to make impact with the center of her chest, she vanishes. "Oh, come on! Where'd she..." Eddie looks around the room for any sign of Lisa before running back to the main stage area. Everyone there is gone, too. No blood. No anything. Just an eerie silence.

Chapter 25

Eddie makes his way out into the street which is now damp with rain. A few of the people from inside the club are running through a light fog toward the diner. He scans the street, searching for Lisa and Perry, and he notices Jennifer and Courtney standing under a nearby awning. As he makes his way to them, Jennifer is the first to speak.

"We got as many out as we could, but he's just so fast."

Eddie doesn't register what Jennifer is telling them, much to Courtney's frustration.

"We saved like half of the people. Perry teleported the rest. He was taking three or four at a time. He'll have an army of over a hundred vampires by sun up."

"Tell us you at least got Lisa. Baby vamps won't be that difficult to kill, but the Ice Queen is a different story." Jennifer asks.

Eddie remains silent.

"Fantastic! Some slayer you are," Courtney scoffs, drawing a look of disapproval from Jennifer.

"He must have teleported her before I could finish her, not that I owe you an explanation."

Before the exchange can get any more heated, a black Lincoln Navigator flies around the corner and screeches to a stop in front of them.

"Get in." Lincoln unlocks the door and waits for the three of them to enter the vehicle. "Where would he be taking them?" he asks as they drive along the river past Heinz Field and PNC Park.

Courtney looks from Lincoln to Jennifer. "How does he...?"

"They share a brain, or something," Jennifer tries to explain and the explanation must be good enough because Eddie and Lincoln don't elaborate.

Courtney relaxes back into the seat. "Nice ride *Lincoln*, even if it is a little vain."

"Thanks. Now, Perry. Where would he go?"

Courtney shrugs and Jennifer exhales a long sad sigh.

"Perry is the oldest, wisest vampire there is. We won't find him. Our best bet is to wait until the newbies start killing and follow their trail back to him."

"That's unacceptable!" Lincoln slams his fist down on the steering wheel. "No more innocent lives—"

"Lincoln, he can be anywhere! I watched him teleport and I have no idea how I'm going to catch him, let alone beat him. Just get us home. We all need some rest." Eddie wraps his arm around Jennifer.

Lincoln opens his mouth, but closes it without speaking and heads back to his apartment.

Chapter 26

October 31, 2016 Uniontown, PA

Perry and Lisa skip arm-in-arm through the mansion, which they confiscated to house their vampire army. They took one hundred and eighteen people that night—fifty-eight new vampires and a feeding partner for each of them. They skip from room to room, checking on each pair, giggling every time they hear a shriek and smiling proudly at each of their offspring's blood covered faces. Most of their chosen have already embraced vampirism and some have even started to display their unique abilities.

Perry has chosen one of Lisa's progeny as a mate, a Latina dancer from the club named Penelope who can stretch her limbs like Silly Putty. They spend most of their time alone in the master suite.

Lisa, after the heartbreak of losing Courtney, opted for something different in the form of a former bouncer at the club named Cedric. Lisa learned of Cedric's ability earlier that morning. He was on top of her and as the excitement began to mount, his power began to manifest. Suddenly Cedric was gone, and Lisa was the wettest she'd ever been. It took twenty minutes for Cedric to figure out how to re-solidify himself, and another hour for Lisa to explain that it's okay, things like that sometimes happen to vampires, and he shouldn't be embarrassed. However, it only took Perry ten seconds after hearing the story to come up with Cedric's new nickname: Puddles.

Besides their respective mates, five others have displayed their unique gifts.

Riley, another former dancer, has been flying around the mansion since about five minutes after she had her first taste of caffeinated blood. Jack, a former bartender whose touch is somehow lethal to other vampires, as evidenced by his accidental killing of two female newbies who he attempted to mate with. Their deaths were slower than any Lisa or Perry had ever witnessed; their hearts and heads turned black, and eventually their bodies turned to ash.

Devin, the female DJ at the club, can lure any human toward her with a song. They had to stop her from stealing the other vampires' humans countless times last night. Then, just this morning, Perry nearly shit himself when he opened his door to find a rattlesnake staring back at him. It's an irrational fear as a snakebite couldn't harm him at all, but something about the rattling sound gets to him. He screamed and Lisa rushed to his rescue, grabbing the snake by the head. Two seconds later, her hand was around the neck of Scott, a customer from the club, who can now shape-shift into any animal.

And finally, Mason, the club owner who sits in front of them now, with his face buried in the neck of one of his former employees. He pauses from feeding but doesn't look up. "Yes, my power has manifested."

Lisa glances at Perry, who raises an eyebrow. "Mason, how did you—"

"I read your mind. And yes, I *am* better in bed then Puddles," he replies before sinking his teeth back into his meal.

Lisa blushes. "I think we can go to battle with just the five and us."

"Maybe." Perry stands at a window and stares out at some of the rolling hills that surround the mansion, preoccupied with his thoughts. Lisa moves to his side. "Did you get Jack the gloves?"

"Yes. He has them." He pauses. "Penelope and Puddles must stay back. They can try to help some of the others develop their gifts. I can't stand losing another mate. The five are very valuable. Maybe we should send ten of the less valuable newbies into the city to see what exactly we're up against."

Lisa scoffs.

"Lisa, that slayer would have killed you had I not come to your rescue. We should *not* take our foes lightly."

"Yes, father."

"Select the ten weakest and have Puddles drive them to the edge of the South Side. Instruct them to come back in two days. We will see how many return and plan our battle strategy accordingly."

Chapter 27

Lincoln's apartment just isn't big enough.

Beth and Noel are asleep in Lincoln's room and Eddie gave up the guest room for Jennifer and Courtney. Lincoln has been spending most of his waking hours scanning the Internet and watching the local news, hoping to find anything that will lead them to Perry and Lisa. Rocko has claimed the couch, leaving Eddie only the recliner to get what little sleep he can, when he isn't scouring the streets hunting for vampires and stopping in every bar along the way to refuel.

"Anything, Lincoln?" he asks hopefully as he plops down in the chair.

"Nada."

"Did he go anywhere else in your story?"

Lincoln hesitates. "The whole story takes place in the city, and Perry is originally from Ireland, where he was a druid. I've been monitoring Irish news sites and there is nothing out of the ordinary." Lincoln again hesitates, then begins to frantically type on his computer.

The Editor

"What? What is it?" Eddie moves quickly to Lincoln's side.

"Lisa. She was from *a small town close to the city, the daughter of a wealthy coal baron,*" his voice is full of excitement. "I need to expand my local search area. Keep hitting the streets, and God willing, I'll find something soon."

Chapter 28

Eddie wanders the cold, windy streets of the South Side hoping to find any signs of a vampire that may lead him back to Perry. He's about to give up for the night when the distant screams reach him. He starts to move in the direction of the screams when his cell phone vibrates in his pocket. He pulls his phone from his pocket, checks the display, and groans.

"Courtney? Not a good time. I think—"

"Well, I *know*," she interjects. "Get down to Rusty's on 11th Street. There's five of them. Shit!"

Eddie stares at his phone for a minute until he realizes that Courtney is no longer on the other end. He closes his eyes and takes a sip of bourbon from the flask that he has started to carry. He pictures Rusty's in his mind. He knows the place well; he's been frequenting it for the past few days while patrolling for vampires. Suddenly, the yelling is louder and he's startled by a crash and the sound of glass breaking nearby.

"How in the world?" He hears Courtney's voice as he opens his eyes to a scene of absolute carnage. Blood covers the walls of Rusty's back room and two vampires have a young man pinned down on the pool table where they are sucking him dry.

Eddie glances briefly at Courtney, who holds a heart in one hand and the head of a female vampire in the other, and shrugs. "Superpowers, I guess."

He pulls two ivory stakes from his inside coat pocket and drives them through the heart of each vampire turning them both to ash. He checks for a pulse, but it's too late to save the man on the table.

"Two more in the front room." Courtney motions toward a door at the far side of the room. "They're all very new. I don't think any have had their powers manifest yet." She follows Eddie as he creeps toward the doorway. The smell of stale beer and day-old popcorn is almost enough to overpower the smell of the blood that covers the floor behind them.

Eddie peers into the front bar of Rusty's. It looks like a laser show gone completely wrong. Charred remains of the vampires' victims are strewn about. A beautiful, scantily clad female vampire is sitting in the far corner laughing euphorically while a skinny male vampire shoots lasers from his mouth in every direction.

Eddie and Courtney slip behind the bar undetected and find the bartender cowering in fear. Eddie holds a finger to his mouth. "It will be okay," he mouths to the older woman who begins to cry softly.

"What're we gonna do, Eddie?" Courtney whispers as she turns to him. Her brow furrows and her mouth hangs agape—she doesn't know whether to be in awe or to be horrified. "Eddie... your skin."

Eddie's eyes fall to his palms and he catches his reflection in them. His skin has taken the form of mirrors. Lincoln must sense his concern.

Use it to your advantage, Eddie. It wouldn't happen if it wasn't beneficial.

Eddie looks back at the bartender. She's fainted, or possibly had a heart attack. Either way, at least she'll stay out of the way. He turns to Courtney. "Do your thing. I just need a second to get into position."

Courtney nods and begins to sing a beautiful song, one that Eddie has never heard before. She slowly climbs out from behind the bar. She has both of the vampire's full attention.

Eddie uses his reflective body to gauge where his enemies are and gets ready to make his move. His heart beats hard against his chest. It's beating so hard that it's difficult for him to swallow. He has a plan, but it requires complete faith in his power, and therefore, complete faith in Lincoln.

The Editor

Both newbie vampires begin to smile with their eyes full of lust as they glide closer to Courtney. As soon as they reach the spot where Eddie wants them, he springs over the bar with the agility of a panther. Courtney stops singing and dives back behind the bar. The male vampire begins a guttural growl and opens his mouth firing a laser in Eddie's direction. Eddie closes his eyes and recoils, angling his hand so that the laser deflects off his mirror-like skin and hits the female vampire, searing a hole in her ample chest.

Thank God. Eddie opens his eyes when he realizes that his plan is working. Before the male vampire can close his mouth, Eddie changes the angle of his hand and sends the laser right back where it came from. The laser hits the back of vampire's throat and he swallows. He stumbles back against a wall, sending a neon sign crashing to the floor. His eyes begin to bulge and he grabs at his throat with both hands. Eddie starts toward him in hopes of finishing him off, but before he reaches him the vampire's head explodes, covering Eddie with blood and brain matter. "Fuckin' disgusting." He nearly vomits as he spits out a molar—not one of his own. Before he can even make it to what was left of the body, Courtney is there, tearing the heart from its chest.

Courtney tosses the heart over her shoulder and it lands at the base of a jukebox. "Shit. That was a scary power."

"Eh," Eddie says between deep breaths, still trying not to puke as his skin returns to normal. "Let's grab the girl and get her back to Lincoln's before she heals. We need to get her to give up Perry's location."

Chapter 29

Thankfully, Lincoln's apartment has its own garage. Eddie carries the seemingly lifeless vampire woman up the steps and drops her on the living room floor. Courtney follows close behind him. Lincoln hands Eddie a glass of Eagle Rare and eyes the vampire at his feet. Her wound has already closed and before long, she'll be awake.

"Drink up." Lincoln nods toward the glass he handed Eddie.

Eddie snorts and finishes the glass in two swallows. "I better not see your ass at my future intervention."

Jennifer smiles wide and puts an arm around both Eddie and Courtney. "It's so nice to see you two working so well together." Eddie swallows the last of his bourbon and mumbles something before starting toward a rare open seat on the couch, but before he makes it there, he hears a gasp and spins around knocking a lamp from an end table.

The female vampire's eyes shoot open and her body begins to vibrate so fast that the house begins to shake. An expensive-looking crystal swan falls from the mantle over the fireplace and breaks into thousands of tiny shards.

Eddie, do something... besides breaking my shit.

Eddie shoots a glare at Lincoln before lifting a hand in the air and slowly clenching it into a fist.

The vampire's head snaps in Eddie's direction. She gasps and her eyes bulge. She begins to choke and finally stops her vibrations.

"Okay, okay, you win," she gasps.

Chapter 30

Lincoln approaches the vampire woman slowly, but deliberately, hands out in front of him, bracing for an attack. She is attractive. *Very* attractive. Strawberry blonde hair covers her shoulders as she lies paralyzed with fear on the floor, her icy blue eyes locked on Eddie, waiting for him to do whatever he had done to her a moment ago, again. The laser had torn a hole through her chest, which has since healed, but the shirt was not as lucky. Lincoln blushes and hands her a blanket to cover her partially exposed breasts.

"What's your name, miss?"

The vampire momentarily breaks her gaze and looks at him. Her eyes narrow. "W-wh-what?"

"It's okay. We don't want to hurt you. If we did, Eddie would have killed you back at Rusty's. We just need information. We need to know where to find Perry and Lisa."

The vampire remains silent, glancing at each of her captors one at a time, trying to gauge if they can be trusted.

Jennifer finally breaks the silence. "Hi, sweetie. I'm Jenny," she extends her hand.

"You're..."

"A vampire, yes. And I believe that you have already met my daughter Courtney." She motions to Courtney who waves sarcastically. "Pretty neat trick you did there with the whole earthquake thing."

"I, uh... it was the first time."

"It's okay, sweetie, we can help you control it. But why don't you start by telling us your name, okay?" Jennifer places what is meant to be a reassuring hand on the other vampire's shoulder.

The new vampire stiffens momentarily, but then slouches back into her seat. "Abby."

"Alright Abby, we know that you can't betray your father, but we need to stop Perry and Lisa before the take any more innocent lives."

"My father died when I was young. I won't betray Lisa, but Perry is a piece of shit. If I could give you him without harming my... mother... I would."

Eddie catches Lincoln's glance.

Perry is who we really need to kill. Once he's gone, maybe we can make Lisa understand.

That's not how it works, Eddie. Unless he releases Lisa like he did Jennifer, or he tries to kill someone that she has imprinted on, she'll try to avenge his death until she meets her own.

"Hi, Abby. My name is Lincoln." He holds out a hand that Abby does not take. After an uncomfortably long period of time Lincoln puts down his hand and continues. "Look, we don't have to hurt anyone. We just have to explain how all of this came about, and why they need to stop killing humans and making more vampires," he says, knowing his attempt to gain her trust is weak.

Abby stares ahead blankly.

"We know where they are, or at least have it narrowed down to three general locations, so you can either tell us now and save some innocent lives, or we can search all three until we find them... and we *will* find them."

Jennifer begins to speak. "Lincoln, you don't understand. She couldn't tell you even if she wanted—"

Lincoln holds up a hand with a sheet of paper in it, and Jennifer pauses.

"We know that they are reasonably close, as they would want to keep tabs on you. We also know that Lisa was the daughter of one of Pittsburgh's coal barons." He pauses, noticing that he has Abby's undivided attention now. "I also know that I should be more specific in any future writing," he mumbles under his breath before continuing. "Knowing Perry's need for luxury, and your need for space and privacy, we have narrowed our search to three properties. Henry Clay Frick's Clayton house in the city, which is unlikely because of the close proximity and heavy population."

Abby doesn't betray even a hint of emotion.

Lincoln goes on. "Linden Hall, former home of Sarah Moore Cochran."

Abby's eyes shift downward and linger on the floor for a second, but when she looks back up, her eyes gleam with curiosity, not fear that her mother is in trouble.

"And finally," Lincoln clears his throat. "Mount St. Macrina in Uniontown, the former home of JV Thompson."

Did you see that? Eddie asks Lincoln through their shared connection.

Yep. This is our place. She recognized the city and her Grandfather's name. Watch this.

"That is before his buddy, the aforementioned Mr. Frick, crushed him and forced him to declare bankruptcy."

Abby winces, as if an ivory stake had just pierced her heart, before she can catch herself.

"After he died, Lisa and her mother had to leave the estate in shame. They were forced to move to a patch town, which is where Perry likely found her."

"JV Thompson was the greatest of all the Pennsylvania coal barons! Frick and Lynch were jealous and they ruined him because of it!" Abby spits back angrily as she begins to shake again. Eddie balls his hand into a fist and she stops, though the angry glare never leaves her face.

"Okay, everyone. We're going to Uniontown." Lincoln grins, ignoring her glare. "Get together what you need. We need to be on the road in half an hour. Beth, we'll be back in time for the memorial." He sounds more hopeful than confident, though.

Chapter 31

The ride to Uniontown is pretty uneventful; boring, even. It's mostly highway once they're out of the city and the highway cuts through empty fields and farms.

"I didn't realize how close we were to leaving civilization." Jennifer laughs quietly while taking Eddie's hand.

Eddie takes a sip from his flask and closes his eyes, just hoping to get to their destination soon. The sooner he can take care of Perry and Lisa, the sooner he and Jennifer can start their lives together.

They follow Lincoln, who's driving Courtney and Abby in his car. He takes an exit to the right, so Rocko follows his lead. "We must be close, Miss Jenny."

Eddie's eyes spring open. They make another right and soon come to Route 40, which is a busier street lined on each side with restaurants, stores, and car dealerships.

"Thank goodness," Jennifer whispers as she takes in all the retail glory.

Eddie gives her a sideways glance. "I don't think we'll have much time for shopping, my love."

Jennifer chuckles. "A girl like me can always make time to shop."

Rocko follows Lincoln as he pulls into a shopping center on the right.

Eddie scans the shopping center trying to find a purpose for the detour. *Lincoln, what in the hell are you doing?*

I'm hungry. We can't go to battle on an empty stomach.

Couple things, Lincoln. First, you aren't going into battle. Second, I can't fight vampires if I'm all bloated.

I didn't say you had to eat, but I am *eating. They have bourbon, you'll be fine.*

"Lincoln wants to eat," Eddie explains to Jennifer and Rocko. Jennifer doesn't even lift her eyes up from her phone.

"Sounds good to me." Rocko pats his belly and pulls into a parking space in front of the restaurant.

Chapter 32

The restaurant is a sports bar; a large chain-type establishment decorated with pictures of local athletes and school sports teams. It's fairly empty, mostly because of the time; too late for lunch, still too early for dinner.

"Do you think it was a good idea to leave Beth and Noel at the apartment?" Courtney asks as everyone crams into a corner booth. "I mean, if Perry finds out where the apartment is..."

"He won't," Lincoln glares directly at Abby. "They'll be fine."

"And does anyone else notice how much Noel—" Jennifer shoots a look at Courtney and she stops mid-sentence as the waitress approaches to take their order. Everyone orders a drink and they order a few appetizers between them. Everyone except Lincoln, who orders a full meal.

As the waitress leaves to put in their order, Lincoln begins to speak. "Okay, we need to be sharp when we approach them."

The Editor

"Again with this *we* shit. You aren't going any-where near them. Courtney will have to stay with Abby, so it will just be Jennifer and me versus the brood. Although, if it was up to me, I'd just end Abby and then Courtney could help us." Eddie smirks at Abby, who begins to tremor before Eddie clenches his fist. Again, Abby loses her breath.

Lincoln glares at Eddie. "We aren't killing Abby. She can be very beneficial to us if she wants to. Courtney can go with you and Jennifer. I'll be fine with Abby."

If she acts up, I'll use our connection to let you know and you can do your fist-clench-steal-her-breath thing, Lincoln mind-speaks to Eddie, who nods subtlety in reply.

The waitress returns with the drinks and appetiz-ers and everyone begins to eat while Lincoln details the rest of the plan.

Chapter 33

Mt. Macrina Manor is set up on a hill, just off the main road that runs through the heart of Uniontown. There are two entrances onto the property, but Eddie, Jennifer, and Courtney don't use either of them. Instead, they park just off a highway that borders a wooded area of the property and approach on foot.

We're in place, Lincoln. Let me know when we should begin our approach.

Lincoln hesitates before answering while he and Abby drive up the long winding driveway toward the main house. He surveys the area, then responds.

There's a graveyard just ahead. Go to the northwest corner and wait there for my signal. You'll be able to see the back of the mansion from there.

Eddie relays the plans to Jennifer and Courtney and they make their way to the graveyard.

Lincoln pulls the car directly in front of a security camera at the front of the house and gets out. He walks around to the passenger side door and opens it for Abby. She takes his hand, gracefully exits the car, and makes her way to the front door. Lincoln follows close behind. Abby pauses momentarily and turns to Lincoln with a look of confusion mixed with sadness. "I...I—" she stutters.

Lincoln pulls Abby in against his chest. "It's okay. You have us."

Eddie, are you in place?

Yes. Should we attack?

No, hold tight. I'm going in.

You're what?!

Chapter 34

Inside the mansion, Perry approaches Lisa, who's sitting in front of a security monitor. He sighs and shakes his head. "Well, you did exactly as the human wanted you to."

"Who cares? She's powerless and she brought *him* here. Releasing her was just shedding dead... *undead* weight." Lisa laughs smugly at her own joke.

Perry raises his eyebrows. "I'm the funny one, dear. And I thought I'd taught you better than that, my darling daughter. No vampire is powerless, and usually the longer it takes a power to manifest, the stronger that power will be. Plus, she hasn't imprinted on the fool. He played you, and he won. Luckily, I am a far better player than you, my child. Instruct Colin to let them in and take them to the grand dining hall. Get them something to eat and drink, and tell them that I'll be with them shortly."

Lisa lowers her head obediently and shuffles over to the phone to call Colin. "My joke wasn't *that* bad," she mumbles as the phone rings in her ear.

Chapter 35

Lincoln? Lincoln! What in the hell is going on?

Relax, Eddie. Everything is under control. We're sitting in the dining hall waiting for Perry.

And what exactly do you plan to do when he gets there?

What do I...? Kill him of course.

As Eddie starts to mentally protest, Abby gasps and Perry appears at the far end of the excessively long banquet table.

"Welcome." Perry speaks calmly, but smiles in a way that allows his fangs to be clearly visible.

Lincoln nods, afraid that a verbal response will betray his nerves.

"Thank you for returning Abigail. Her mother..."

Abigail shudders at the term as she knows that she is no longer bonded to Lisa in any way.

"...her mother will be delighted." Perry smiles kindly at the young vampire. She shudders again.

Lincoln clears his throat. "Returning her? No, I think you have the wrong idea. I came to claim *my* creations."

Intrigue then anger flashes across Perry's face. He quickly masks his emotions with another smile. "*Your* creations, human? This should be good. Go on. Who are *your* creations?" He motions for Lincoln to explain.

"Well, really just you and Lisa, but I'll take responsibility for the rest, too, since they all spawned from you two."

"How big of you." Perry laughs. "Only one problem with that, oh mighty creator. I'm a few millennia older than you. I was created by the original vampire and *you* are not *her*." He lets out another smug chuckle.

"Yeah? What did she look like? What do you remember of your life before being turned into a vampire? Where is the original vampire now?"

The ancient vampire sits silently and stares at Lincoln, waiting for an explanation. Lincoln grins confidently, knowing that Perry cannot answer his questions and that he has begun to realize that he may not be exactly what he thinks he is.

Lincoln reaches into his coat pocket and pulls a few pages of bound paper from his pocket. He slides them down the table to Perry who curiously picks them up and begins to scan them.

"Sound familiar? Check the time stamp. Long before our paths crossed on this world. You're a figment of my imagination, somehow brought to life."

"This is nonsense!" Perry crumbles the papers and throws them back at Lincoln.

"I thought you might say that." Lincoln's voice remains calm as he removes his laptop from his case and sets it on the table. After a few short keystrokes, an ivory stake appears on the table.

"Oh, a tough guy? Is that a threat?" Perry bares his fangs.

"No, Perry. *That* is proof." Lincoln smirks back raising his hands in mock surrender.

Apparently, Perry has seen enough because he suddenly vanishes.

Eddie, approach the back door and be ready to attack.

Chapter 36

Lincoln and Abby watch as Perry's brood of vampires, led by Lisa, file into the room from multiple entrances and surround them. Lincoln inhales deeply and slowly, willing himself to remain calm.

"This is going to be a *chilling* experience for you two." Lisa laughs as she steps toward Abby and Lincoln.

"That was cute. Sort of like your *cute* little freezing power, Mom," Abby mocks.

Lisa's eyes narrow. "Coming from a powerless, disowned *bitch*."

Lincoln glances at Abby and smirks. Abby raises a hand releasing a wave of heat that causes the entire brood of vampires to take a step back.

"That was new." Lincoln smiles at Abby who returns his smile with a grin of her own.

Suddenly, the male vampire standing next to Lisa liquefies and shoots towards them like a tidal wave. Abby holds up both hands and the heat she produces causes Lincoln to step back, even though the bulk of it is focused on the wave headed in their direction.

The Editor

Lincoln braces himself for the impact of the wave, but it never comes.

"Puddles?" Lisa cries frantically. "Puddles! Where are you?"

"Humid in here all of the sudden, huh?" Abby exaggerates a wipe of her forehead. "Makes my hair so frizzy."

"Bitch! You evaporated my mate!" Lisa begins to move toward Abby.

Before Abby can raise her hand to send a heat wave Lisa's way, another vampire grabs Lisa's shoulder.

"It's okay, Lisa. He'll eventually condense back into form."

"Interesting theory." Abby smirks. "One that might have been true, had I not removed his head and heart." She steps aside, revealing Puddle's head and heart on the floor behind her.

Lisa's eyes move from the floor, to Abby, and then to her progeny.

An eerie calm falls over her before she speaks. "Kill them. *Slowly*."

Chapter 37

Gonna need some help quick, Eddie.

The vampires begin to run toward Lincoln and Abby, but just as they are about to reach them, they are blown back with hurricane force winds. All the windows in the room burst causing enough of a distraction that Eddie, Jennifer, and Courtney can enter undetected.

Lisa smirks. "Impressive. I guess I was hasty releasing you."

Another vampire moves to Lisa's left side. "Mother, there are others here. I heard the human thinking about someone coming to their rescue."

"Thank you, Mason." Lisa looks around the room. Her former lover, Courtney, Jennifer, and Eddie have spread out forming a semi-circle in front of her, preparing for a fight.

"Jack, take the brown-haired female." A wiry male begins to stalk toward Jennifer. Eddie takes a step in Jack's direction before Lisa speaks again. "I'm sure she'll love the way you touch her." She smiles directly at Eddie before she continues. "Riley and Scott, take the hunter. Don't underestimate him."

A beautiful raven-haired female shoots up into the air like a rocket and hovers above Eddie. The largest of the male vampires suddenly drops to all fours and begins to grow even bigger until his leather jacket splits in two and brown hair begins to sprout from his back and arms. His face twists in pain, before elongating into a snout of some sort.

With Eddie's attention drawn to the transformation in front of him, the flying vampire swoops down and strikes him in the back, knocking him to his knees. His vision goes in and out and a high-pitched whistle echoes in his ears until a thunderous growl brings him back to full consciousness. He gets to his feet and stares face-to-face with the largest grizzly bear that he has ever seen.

Lisa laughs and turns to a female who looks like the lead singer of a punk rock band. "Devin, just do your thing to the human. Mason, you stick close to me. Abby is ours. The rest of you, bring me the black-haired female. Alive."

Vampires shoot off in every direction. Jack is no match for Jennifer's speed. She giggles as she avoids him easily, while still killing a few of the newbies that Courtney is holding off by making them lust for her.

Lincoln grabs the edge of a heavy marble end table, trying to fight the urge to move toward Devin, who is singing an annoying pop song. He's fighting a losing battle. Lincoln's knuckles turn white, as he does his best to keep from moving toward her. His fingers begin to slip.

Abby sends a gust of wind through the room that whips Riley against a wall. A few of Courtney's suitors are also blown to the ground where Jennifer makes quick work of them.

Lisa runs toward Abby with Mason close behind. The ground shakes so violently that everyone is forced to stop fighting momentarily. The floor cracks open directly in front of Lisa, but she's agile enough to leap over the fault. Mason isn't as lucky. Lisa continues towards Abby, her hands glowing an icy blue. Abby's eyes turn deep orange and she opens her mouth, spewing a bright-red liquid in Lisa's direction. Lisa recoils and retreats behind a table that was knocked over by the tremors. Abby continues to spew the lava into the fault until it's like a red river dividing the room in two.

Eddie, I could use a little help here.

Yeah, right after I sprout some wings, kill a flying vampire, and tame the world's largest grizzly bear.

Lincoln is almost in Devin's grasp. The attraction is unexplainable. She's not his type, but the closer he gets, the more he wants to just give in to her. When the urge to resist becomes too great and he caves, both physically and mentally, what looks like a lightning bolt flies by him and hits the pink-haired, purple-eyed vampire in her leather-clad chest. She's knocked back against the wall stopping her song, and Lincoln's attraction, mid-chorus.

"Thank God. I *hate* that song." Jennifer slows down long enough to give Abby a high-five. "Can I adopt you? You're pretty badass, girl!"

The bear formerly known as Scott springs forward at Eddie who rolls out of the way but suddenly feels a sharp pain behind his shoulder blades. His back arches and his head is thrown back violently. He screams in pain, thinking that the bear has dug its paws into his back, but opens his eyes to find both the bear and Riley staring at him in horror. The pain stops as suddenly as it came on and he gets to his feet. He can feel everyone's eyes on him.

Your natural form. The voice in his head is unfamiliar, not his and not Lincoln's. He doesn't have time to question whose voice it is, though. He quickly becomes aware of the wings on his back, and as if it were as natural as breathing, he takes flight and heads toward Riley. She does all that she can to avoid him—darting left, then right, then looping backwards. When he follows her into a loop, Eddie notices a quiver full of ivory-tipped arrows hanging on his back. The bow that somehow appears in his left hand, seems to be made of pure light.

The vampires all shield their eyes from the bow's light.

Nice touch, he thinks as he flies over to Lincoln to make sure that he's okay.

That one... wasn't me.

He can see that Lincoln isn't in any immediate danger so he takes aim at a few of the newbies. Courtney seems to be having trouble holding them off, but Eddie drops them with ease. No matter how many arrows he shoots, his quiver seems to always be full. He looks for Jennifer but she's moving so fast that he can't find her. The distraction is all Riley needs to swoop in and knock him off his feet again.

The bear is quick to pounce on his prey and uses a giant paw to knock Eddie against the wall. He drops his bow, disoriented. The taste of iron fills his mouth as he tries to get to his feet. The room spins and he falls back down to one knee. The sounds of battle are now muted and he can't seem to regain his balance. The muffled growls of the bear grow louder, and soon its hot breath is sticky against the side of his face. He turns his head just as the open jaw of the bear quickly comes down toward his neck. Then everything goes black.

Chapter 38

Is this hell? It can't be Heaven, it's dark and it smells horrible. Eddie's stomach drops, as he fears that he's stuck in some sort of purgatory. He hadn't thought about Heaven or Hell much previously, but sprouting wings and holding a bow made of pure light is enough to make anyone ponder the subject. It's obvious to him now that both exist. Maybe since he was not created traditionally, he doesn't get to go to either, but is instead stuck in this dark place that stinks of stale beer and raw fish.

Eddie? Can you hear me?

Lincoln? Are you dead, too?

Dead? No. Not yet anyway. You just disappeared when the bear snapped at you. Where are you?

I... I don't know. Somewhere terrible.

Then it happens; the dark world around Eddie begins to shake violently and an explosion shoots him forward into a ball of light.

When he regains his composure, he realizes that he's not dead. In fact, he's not even injured. He's back in the room, but it's somehow different—bigger. Lincoln is to his right and he's also bigger. As a matter of fact, he's a giant.

Lincoln, what happened. Why are you so huge?

Huge? I mean I've been working out some, but I wouldn't classify myself as huge. Where are you?

What do you mean? I'm flying right in front of you.

Huh? Oh... my...

Lincoln, what is it, damnit?

Well, I guess you didn't disappear after all. You just... shapeshifted. You're a... fly.

Eddie looks down at himself and finds the hairy black body of a flying insect.

How am I supposed to fight vampires as a fly?

Can't you change yourself back, or into something that can kill a bear? What can kill a bear? A lion, or maybe a rhino?

Hey, asshole, I didn't purposefully change myself into a freaking fly, but I may have an idea. If I can figure out how to change myself back.

It seems that when you need to change, you do. So just give it a shot.

Eddie flies back in the direction of the bear, careful to avoid anything or anyone that may inadvertently squash him. He circles behind the beast, which frantically moves its head in every direction trying to find out what happened to its meal.

Here goes nothing, Eddie thinks as he wills himself to shift back into his normal form.

The bear is suddenly back to being just regular huge, and when Eddie looks down, he finds the legs and feet of a human— or angel, but definitely not a fly. He reaches into his belt for something he thought he'd never use and shoves it into what he hopes is the bear's anus and squeezes. At first the bear just pauses curiously, but soon its eyes widen and it begins to snort and growl in agony. It takes a step forward, then stumbles and falls on its side. The once formidable beast, now helpless, stares directly into Eddie's eyes, as if pleading for him to stop whatever he's started. It continues growling as it writhes in pain for a few moments, then stops abruptly.

Eddie begins to approach the bear but then it twitches violently three times, and dissolves into a large pile of ashes. He stares at the pile in disbelief.

You are a sick son of a bitch, Lincoln.

Chapter 39

"Hmmm. I guess that isn't just a vampiric urban legend after all," Jennifer muses as she tears a newbie's head off and rips out its heart before racing away from Jack again.

Riley, who has been releasing an ear-bursting shriek ever since the decaf enema, dives toward Eddie. He readies himself for her attack, but it never comes. Instead, she veers off to her right striking Jennifer mid-sprint and knocking her against a wall.

Courtney can sense the danger that her mother now faces. She's distracted, and the lack of concentration is all the newer vampires need to overpower her.

Eddie, help.

Eddie hears the mind-speak as though it was a whisper and turns left, then right, until he finds Lincoln's motionless body lying against the remains of one of the dining chairs. Devin is lurking over him, blood dripping from her fangs. Eddie's pulse quickens and his breathing suddenly becomes more difficult. Their defeat is imminent.

He closes his eyes briefly in an attempt to gain the clarity needed to choose which of his allies to rescue: Courtney or Lincoln? As he blinks his eyes open again, a blinding light fills the room. All the vampires cower, shielding their faces. Only after noticing that they are all cowering away from *him*, does he realize that the light is coming from him; from his wings, to be exact.

Eddie grabs an ivory-tipped arrow from his quiver and fires it directly through Devin's chest and a pile of ash rains down over Lincoln's body. Lincoln scrambles to wipe the ashes from his face and frantically starts to spit, attempting to clear his mouth of the former DJ.

Abby sends a blast of wind across the room that knocks Lisa against the far wall. Lisa slowly gets to her feet and scrambles out the door from which they entered. Abby begins her pursuit, but before she can take a second step, Riley stealthily lands behind her and rips her head from her body. Lincoln finally makes it to his feet and hurls the arrow that destroyed Devin toward Riley like a mini javelin, striking her in the arm and forcing her to drop Abby's body.

Riley cries out in pain and takes off toward the exit. She alters direction mid-flight, though, and swoops into the crowd of newbies, plucking Courtney into the air before heading back toward the exit. At that same moment, Jack bears down on Jennifer, who still isn't moving. Eddie has a choice to make. Will he save Jennifer or Courtney? His soulmate, or her vampiric daughter?

Eddie grabs an arrow from his quiver and closes his eyes. His heart races and a wave of nausea roils through him. When he opens his eyes, he sends an arrow across the room. The arrow finds its mark, going straight through Jack's back and piercing his heart. Jack's body falls lifelessly onto Jennifer before turning to ash. Eddie whips back around toward the door, ready to fire another arrow, but the room is empty, save for what remains of his once surprisingly formidable team.

Chapter 40

"Not a bad throw, man." Eddie pats Lincoln on the back.

"Yeah, I threw javelin in high school." Lincoln taps his foot nervously, but his eyes don't leave Abby's headless body.

"You tried." Eddie tries to sound comforting, but Lincoln just gives him a puzzled stare.

A horrific choking sound comes from Jennifer's direction. Eddie stops any further consoling and rushes to her side.

"Babe, are you okay?" He drops to his knees and cradles her head. She doesn't speak, but the terror in her eyes tells him that she is anything but okay. She glances to her left, and Eddie's eyes follow hers to what looks like a bloody handprint that covers her bare shoulder. Eddie smiles weakly and uses his sleeve to wipe at the handprint. When he pulls the sleeve away the handprint remains, in fact, it becomes an even darker shade of red, almost purple.

"His hand must have hit her before he disintegrated completely." Now it's Lincoln's turn at an attempt to comfort. He kneels next to Jennifer and keeps his face shielded from Eddie as long as he can.

"What do I do, man?" Eddie's voice shakes, the mark now almost black.

"I... I don't—"

"Blood. She needs blood. It won't cure her, but it may buy us some time," a female calls out confidently from behind them.

"Abby!" Lincoln spins around excitedly as Eddie stares at her in disbelief. "Riley didn't get her heart." Lincoln motions towards Abby as she bears her fangs and rips into Eddie's arm. Once she's drawn blood, Abby presses his arm firmly against Jennifer's mouth to make sure that it makes it into her system.

"Holy blood!" Abby closes her eyes as she licks the excess from her lips. "There's no caffeine in that stuff, but it's freakin' delicious. I feel incredible for a girl who just got my head ripped off, literally."

As the blood trickles into her mouth, the mark on Jennifer's arm quickly goes from black to purple, and from every shade of red, dark to pink, before finally disappearing. Her eyes shoot open and her back arches.

Eddie jerks his arm back in shock when her eyes pop open. "Honey, are you okay?"

Jennifer beams at her soulmate. "My angel," she whispers as her eyes flutter around the room. "Where's Courtney?"

Chapter 41

"What do you mean *they* have her?!"

Eddie wraps his arms around Jennifer before he responds, partly to comfort her, but mostly to keep her arms confined so that she can't hit him.

"You were hurt, maybe even dying. I could only save one of you at the time." He pulls her in against his chest.

"You made the wrong choice." Jennifer sobs into his shoulder. Eddie's scent, which she could best describe as sunshine with hints of cinnamon. causes her body to relax, even if she doesn't want it to, and soon the tears stop. "So, what do we do?"

"We get her back, of course," Eddie says with the confidence of a warrior who doesn't know the taste of defeat.

Lincoln clears his throat. "But first we search the mansion. Maybe they left clues that will tell us where they're headed. Perry was gone long before Lisa and her crew. They must have had an escape plan in place. Abby and I will search downstairs, and you two look around upstairs, then we'll head back to Pittsburgh and plan our attack."

"You better call Beth and Noel. Tell them to stay in the house and not to invite *anyone* in. And tell them NOT to leave that apartment without us," Jennifer warns, sounding a little more like her normal, confident self.

"You're right." Lincoln nods and walks away while punching the buttons on his cell phone.

Eddie and Jennifer head upstairs, while Abby waits for Lincoln to finish his call.

"They're okay." He smirks shyly at Abby as he disconnects the call. "Beth is pissed that we may be late for the memorial, so we need to get back ASAP. Search the place thoroughly, but quickly," Lincoln says, sounding relieved and nervous at the same time.

"And I'm okay, thanks to you." Abby kisses Lincoln softly on the cheek. He blushes, but then frowns.

"Oh, I'm sorry. I just..." Abby begins.

"No, no, no! You can kiss me any time. I mean... never mind," he stammers back. Abby giggles as she watches him struggle.

Lincoln is actually quite fond of Abby and had hoped that a kiss would prove them soul-mates, just as Eddie and Jennifer's had done.

Maybe it has to be on the lips.

Yeah, maybe, Eddie thinks back sarcastically.

Lincoln gazes at Abby longingly. *Or maybe I just can't get a break.*

You did just survive a battle with the vampire version of the X-men.

Lincoln frowns again and rubs his head as if he could wipe Eddie out of it and heads to the next room. "Follow me. I doubt there's much left intact that could help us in here."

Abby scans the room and is confronted with the disaster that she caused pretty much single-handedly. The lava has started to harden, and what is left of the dining room table and chairs are strewn about. An expensive looking painting that once donned the wall is now impaled on a sculpture of a nude woman, making it look like she is wearing a rectangular skirt. She laughs and calls after Lincoln. "Right behind you."

Chapter 42

The first room that Lincoln and Abby enter is the kitchen, and after a few minutes of rummaging through some drawers and cabinets, they determine that there's nothing that can help them there and they move into a large sitting room. On a coffee table, sits a laptop, which Lincoln opens and promptly scans the browser history. "I see he checked up on my story."

Abby joins Lincoln at the computer which currently displays a list of websites. He clicks the mouse on the fourth address down and a page reviewing Lincoln's online story about vampires who only drink caffeinated blood comes up.

"Wow, I hope someone drains the jerk who wrote this review." Abby rests her head on Lincoln's shoulder, causing his stomach to tighten. She grins as she listens to his blood travel from his heart to a certain extremity.

"Yeah." He laughs as he turns his head and catches a whiff of her, somehow still amazing-smelling hair.

"It really wasn't my best work though." He returns his eyes to the computer screen and continues to search the browser history. "This isn't good."

"What are those?" Abby asks as she scans the words on the screen.

"That's a list of everything that I've written. There's a chance that everything, or at least everything since Perry's story, has come to life," he answers while simultaneously calling Eddie to join them mentally.

"Well, that may be good news then. Did you write about any more heroes like Eddie?"

Lincoln buries his face in his hands. "I was in a dark place." Is all that he can manage before Eddie and Jennifer come jogging down the stairs.

"Hey, we found a library and they must've even had one or two of your books." Eddie holds up what looks like the title sheet to Lincoln's first novel, from the best-selling series *Morals*.

"Had?" Lincoln asks.

"Yeah, this was pinned to the desk with a knife. The library was alphabetized, and there were a few spaces where your name would've fit. I guess Perry is a fan of your work. Not so much of you, though. He changed the title to *MorTals* and added *RIP* before your name." Eddie hands Lincoln the sheet.

"Cute. Well, we have what we need. So, let's go," Lincoln closes the laptop and carries it with him to the front door.

Eddie eyes the vampires and shrugs. "Can we at least get something to eat... or more importantly, drink first? I'm drained."

"There's bourbon in the car. You can finish it on the way to the memorial... however illegal that may be."

Chapter 43

The team minus Courtney returns to Lincoln's apartment and finds Beth and Noel curled up asleep on Lincoln's couch. Lincoln gently shakes Beth to wake her. "Beth, the service," he says, urgency in his voice.

Beth springs up off the couch. "Shit! After all this planning, I'm gonna mess it all up by being late!" She buries her face in Lincoln's chest as the tears begin to flow.

"It's okay. You still have time. The church is only a few blocks away. Just go get dressed and Jennifer can help Noel get ready. She's super fast, remember?"

Lincoln's warm smile calms Beth enough that she heads into the bedroom and reemerges a few minutes later, ready to go. Jennifer dresses Noel in a black dress and ties her hair up in an elegant bun.

"Where did that dress come..." Beth starts before Jennifer's smile answers her question. Beth nods politely as she grabs Noel's hand and hurries out of the apartment.

The service is beautifully planned, considering all that Beth has had on her mind. The church is filled with daffodils, which Beth tearfully explains were Sara's favorite. A string quartet plays the music, and the Reverend gives a very moving eulogy, as apparently, he knew Sara well. All of Beth's co-workers come, except her boss who stayed and worked the bar by himself so that the staff could attend and support their friend. The rest of the church is filled with locals, who in some way or another knew Sara or Beth. Beth and Noel have no family left, so Lincoln, Eddie, Jennifer, and Abby fill the pew next to them.

After the service and a small dinner that follows, the group makes their way out of the church to head back to the apartment.

Beth turns to Jennifer as they leave the church social hall. "So, vampires..."

"Yes, we can go to church. Most of us are actually quite religious," Jennifer explains.

"Thanks for your help today, Jennifer. Noel looks beautiful. That dress..."

"It's the least I could do. It was *my* family..." Jennifer's eyes shift to the ground.

Tears well up in Beth's eyes. "Yes, and I'm not sure that we'll ever be friends, but I don't blame *you*."

The Editor

When they get back to Lincoln's, Beth and Noel both crash back onto the couch, physically and emotionally exhausted. Lincoln covers them with a blanket and motions for the others to follow him to the rooftop balcony.

"Talk fast. It's freakin' cold up here." Jennifer blows in her hands as she takes in the view of the Pittsburgh skyline and the river below it. Eddie wraps his arms around her, filling her with a sense of warmth that is rarely experienced by humans, let alone vampires.

"Yeah, I guess the whole *vampires don't get cold* theory was a load of B.S." Abby shivers as she wraps herself in an embrace. Watching Jennifer and Eddie sends pangs of jealousy through her. She shifts her gaze to Lincoln, longing in her heart.

Lincoln shuffles his feet and clears his throat.

"The book series Perry left as a threat contained enough good to counteract and defeat the abundant evil. It was also not written on this laptop and much of it took place in the town that we just left. We would've noticed if characters from that series were alive." He clears his throat again as the others wait for him to make his point.

"My point is, using that particular story was just to send me a message—he's going to use my characters to kill me."

"We could always make it harder for him to do that." Abby shyly lifts her eyes to meet his.

"Making me a vampire won't solve our problems. We still need to know where Perry is headed and who he's after. When I was looking at the history on his computer, I saw that he viewed pages about three of my lesser known titles. One was set in Greenville, South Carolina—"

"I vote we start there. I love the beach." Jennifer's chin quivers as she speaks, prompting Eddie to pull her closer against his chest again.

"It's on the west side of the state about three hours from the beach, but admittedly warmer than it is here. I doubt that's where he'd go first, though. The book was about a black man who sold out other blacks to the Klu Klux Klan. While he *is* undoubtedly evil, the other two places had villains with more... power."

Eddie throws his hands up in frustration. "Damnit, Lincoln. The girls are freezing and I'm not exactly warm myself. Where are we headed?"

"Well, my guess would be Turks and Caicos. I wrote about a band of ghost pirates there, and a quick Internet search shows that they are most likely alive-*ish*. Ships are being robbed and mysterious things are happening on the islands. If I was starting a war, ghost pirates would be a pretty solid ally."

"So, who fought them? Who should we look for when we get to the islands?" Eddie asks.

"That's just it. They won in the book. There was no hero, they took whoever and whatever they wanted. Probably why the book didn't sell."

"Greeeeat, sounds fun. Ghostbusting with no way to bust ghosts." Eddie shakes his head in disgust.

"Eddie, if you have bourbon, you have what you need. Man, that sounds silly when I say it out loud. But it's true."

"And the other place? Just in case." Jennifer asks.

"Dublin." A voice says from the doorway leading back to the apartment. As everyone turns toward her, Beth tosses Lincoln her cell phone.

"Damnit." Lincoln tosses the phone back to Beth and buries his face in his hands.

"What? Did you write about a gang of rogue dinosaurs with nuclear weapons in Dublin?" Eddie laughs.

"I was hoping Perry would pick quantity over quality. But he's smart. Too damn smart."

Beth hands Eddie the phone. A headline about two people being completely drained of blood outside a Dublin coffee shop shows on the display.

"So, who's in Dublin, Lincoln?"

"Adam and Evil," he mumbles as his eyes shift to

the ground. "They're a little like you, except they only need one bite of an apple to get their powers."

Eddie shakes his head. "Of course. At least it wasn't apple juice."

"Check out the next page." Beth takes the phone back and pulls it up for Eddie.

Bulletproof Modern-Day Bonnie and Clyde Walk Through Vault Door to Rob Bank of Ireland.

"One bite of an apple and these two become invincible bank robbers, and I basically have to have a bourbon IV so that I can give a *bear-pire* an enema. You couldn't have just made me get my powers because my alien DNA reacts weird to Earth's atmosphere or something?"

"I'm a writer, Eddie. I wanted a more interesting antihero."

"You're an idiot, and because you're an idiot, I need a drink."

Chapter 44

Everyone makes their way back down into the apartment. Noel is still peacefully asleep on the couch.

"Don't worry about her, she can sleep through anything." Beth smiles as she readjusts a blanket over her niece.

Eddie pours himself a drink as the others take seats in the living room.

"I'm going to Dublin tonight. I need to get Courtney back. But I also think someone should go to Turks and Caicos and keep an eye on the ghost pirates. Perry with that army behind him is extra scary." Jennifer's matter-of-fact tone doesn't leave much room for argument.

"I agree." Lincoln nods, almost surprised that he and Jennifer agree. "I think you and Eddie should go to Dublin. Abby and I will take Beth and Noel to Turks. Abby's *talents* with the weather should be enough to keep the pirates at bay, literally." Lincoln laughs at his own joke.

Eddie rolls his eyes. "So, seems like we could use some reinforcements. Can you *type us up* some help?"

Eddie motions towards Lincoln's laptop.

"I tried on the way home. Nothing happened. I'll keep trying though. You and Jennifer make quite a formidable team, even without any help, so I have confidence that you'll stop Perry and his crew before any real damage is done." *Just keep me in the loop.* He nods at Eddie.

You do the same. And I want first class tickets to Dublin. It's a long flight.

Lincoln gives Eddie a sideways glance and punches a few buttons on his laptop. "Okay, Eddie and Jennifer need to get to the airport. Your flight leaves at five forty-five so you'll need to head to the airport shortly. We'll leave tomorrow morning and should be at the resort by 3:00 p.m. I booked a place that Noel will love; lots of kids' activities." He looks down at the little girl, who had repositioned herself in her sleep so that she was now snuggled up against him.

"I'm ready." Jennifer suddenly appears in the doorway with three large bags of luggage. Everyone stares at her, mouths open. "What? You know that I'm fast."

"Yeah, but we aren't *moving* to Dublin." Eddie gets out of his chair and heads to his room to pack a bag. He reemerges a few minutes later with a duffel bag and a coat. "Let's go, lassie."

Chapter 45

Eddie and Jennifer get through airport security and board the plane fairly easily using Lincoln and Beth's expired passports and a bit of vampire glamour. They find their seats in first class and watch as the rest of the plane fills to near capacity. A male flight attendant named Dennis brings them drinks— bourbon for Eddie and a Bloody Mary for Jennifer— and does his best to make them completely comfortable prior to takeoff.

"You should probably get some sleep on the flight, sweetie. Perry doesn't need much help to cause problems, and from the sounds of it, we'll need all that we have to beat these guys."

Jennifer leans her head on Eddie's shoulder. Eddie swallows the last of his bourbon and signals to Dennis that he'd like another.

A chill runs down Eddie's neck and the hair on his left arm stands up. An odd sensation washes over him, but he can't place what it is. He scans the first-class cabin, looking for signs of danger. Besides the two of them, there is a family of four, each with their own form of electronic entertainment, none paying a bit of attention to any of the others. Behind them is a large man in an expensive suit wearing a wedding ring. Beside him is a thin, yet almost comically busty woman with a hand on his leg. Eddie notices that *she* is not wearing a ring and shakes his head disapprovingly.

A young couple, presumably on their honeymoon, sits across from the alleged adulterers. Eddie laughs under his breath. Across from Eddie and Jennifer, a young man with large headphones and clothes three sizes too big is already asleep, head against the window. Next to him is a petite woman; her face is plain but pretty. She's not provocatively dressed but it's easy to see that she has a lean, shapely body. She smiles warmly at Eddie, who nods in return, but grabs Jennifer's hand at the same time. The four people in the row behind them seem to be a marketing team headed to Dublin to win a contract with Guinness. And the last row is filled by an elderly couple and, presumably, their grandchildren— a young boy and girl— who, Eddie must admit, are well-behaved for their age.

"What's wrong, sweetie?" Jennifer squeezes Eddie's hand in return.

"Nothing, my love. Just a weird feeling. Maybe it's just flying." He finishes his second drink and closes his eyes.

Chapter 46

The uneasy feeling never really goes away, but the flight lands in Dublin without a hitch. Because of the uneasy feeling, Eddie didn't want to discuss any plans on the plane, so the time on the flight was largely spent getting to know more about each other's pasts. Both Eddie and Jennifer found this a little silly— as their pasts prior to a few weeks ago are fiction— but they still shape who they are, so they figured... *why not.* They did have over six hours to kill, after all.

Eddie learned that Jennifer was plucked, by Perry, from the French court where she was one of Mary, Queen of Scot's, ladies in waiting. She was quite popular in court and made friends easily, which even helped make Mary a bit more popular with the French. Soon after Perry took her from her friend (and took the life of Mary's husband, King Charles), the Queen went back to Scotland and was eventually imprisoned and beheaded.

During this time, Jennifer was still a newly-turned vampire; she and Perry had yet to find that caffeine in the blood helped to curtail their hunger. She would lurk around battles, feeding off wounded soldiers who had no chance of recovery, or sometimes she would hide in the shadows of villages waiting for drunken men who beat their wives or children to stumble by.

She had no real connection to anyone besides Perry during this time and almost forgot about her previous life, until one day she happened upon an execution. She didn't see it happen, but she smelled the blood and pushed her way through the crowd as an almost uncontrollable hunger coursed through her body. As she made her way to the front, she saw the head lying on the ground, separated from its body.

As she looked upon the face—the empty stare coming back at her was that of her friend, the former queen— the hunger left her, and her humanity returned. From that point on, she'd feed when need be, but never again did she kill for food. In fact, she had only killed (without making them a vampire) one human since that day. Sixteen years later, she finally worked her way into Queen Elizabeth's court—and bedchamber—and avenged the Queen of Scots.

It wasn't until the sixteenth century, when the Persian Shah Abbas sent the Persian Embassy to Europe that they discovered the benefits of caffeinated blood. Jennifer took a lover from the Embassy, and he raved and raved about how coffee helped him focus and kept him from falling asleep on his long journeys. She tried to drink the beverage with him and found it disgusting, but also that it helped her extend the period between blood feedings. Eventually, his caffeinated blood began to sing to her from inside his veins, and she could no longer resist the urge to feed on him.

Once she tasted the blood, she knew that she would never again desire un-caffeinated blood. Soon after, she began to display her advanced speed. She also found that after each feeding she could go weeks without another. Perry became curious and eventually she confessed her secret to her vampiric father.

Perry, assuming it was the person and not the caffeinated blood, drained her lover in front of her. Jennifer was crushed, but could not leave because of their bond. To make it up to her, Perry made David as a potential mate for Jennifer, but David was never more than a friend to her. He was way too whiny and was never able to keep up with her— literally and figuratively. It wasn't until Perry allowed her to take the sickly young daughter of a Seventeenth-century German composer— and friend— as her own, that she forgave him. She nursed Christiana Sophia back to health and raised the girl until the age of twenty-six. It was then that they decided to make her into Jennifer's vampiric daughter, and changed her name to Courtney.

Eddie's history is not quite as detailed, probably because Lincoln rushed to write it. He tells Jennifer about how he was orphaned at an early age, how he has no recollection of any family, and has had very few friends in his lifetime, but somehow, he's always had what he needed to survive.

He ran away from a Boston orphanage at the age of twelve, traveled down the Eastern Seaboard and secretly boarded a freight ship that took him to Spain. He traveled through most of Europe and Asia where he was always provided for by kind strangers. He learned many languages and customs. He finally found a home in Korea at the school of Tang Soo Do Moo Duk Kwan. There he found his mentor and first father figure, Hwang Kee. He began to study the art of Tang Soo Do and became quite good at hand-to-hand combat. He also picked up weapons skills rather easily.

Hwang Kee took a special interest in his training, almost from day one. Meditation was the hardest part of his studies; he found that he meditated better after drinking a shot of whiskey, much to his mentor's dis-approval. Once Eddie finally mastered meditation it became clear to him that he was in some way special.

The Editor

He could visualize his enemies' next move— both on and off the battlefield.

He didn't truly find out how or why he was special until 2002, though.

Hwang Kee had just passed away. Eddie's emotions were high and a sparring tournament was being held to honor the father of Tang Soo Do. Eddie wanted nothing more than to honor his mentor by winning the tournament. Eddie breezed through the competition, rarely ever catching a clean blow and ending each fight quickly. His competitors' jealousy had always been evident, but never so much as that day.

The final match pitted Eddie against Kwan Kang-Kuk, his biggest rival. As was his personal custom (and secret from everyone else), Eddie took his pre-match shot of whisky. That day it was from a bottle of cheap bourbon that burned all the way down to his ankles. As the match started, Eddie waited patiently for Kwan to attack and easily side-stepped the kick and connected with a roundhouse to the head, followed by a back kick that knocked Kwan off his feet. Anger boiled inside Kwan as tears filled his eyes. Eddie bowed as he got to his feet in a show of respect, but Kwan charged him wildly, pulling a short blade from somewhere inside his do bak.

As Eddie rose from his bow, Kwan lunged forward, ramming the blade against his abdomen. Much to both Eddie and Kwan's surprise, the blade did not penetrate his skin. Instead, it snapped, falling harmlessly to the ground with a clatter. Eddie reacted first, grabbing Kwan's arm and hip tossing him to the ground. After the change in position, the referee saw the blade on the ground and the base of the knife still in Kwan's hand. They disqualified him, making Eddie the tournament champion.

After honoring his mentor with the victory, Eddie had no reason to remain in Korea. He had no real friends left there, so he decided to book a flight back to the U.S. He enlisted in the army and eventually became a ranger. He served valiantly for years until a mix-up in the Middle East was unfairly pinned on him, leading to a dishonorable discharge. From there, the drinking became worse; he opened a business as a private detective and became a bit of a womanizer. Most of his cases were women who wanted to catch their husband cheating. Once Eddie found proof, it usually led to the wife spending a night or two in his bed; something that he's not proud of.

As they leave the plane, Eddie turns to Jennifer. "So, does it make it true, now? Did you really kill Queen

Elizabeth the first? Now that you are real, does it make *that* real?"

Jennifer just laughs. "I hope not. I mean the bitch deserved it, but I've always somewhat regretted stooping to that level. None of that really matters, now; we have *waaaay* more pressing things to worry about at the moment."

Chapter 47

At baggage claim, they retrieve Jennifer's many checked bags and then they head to find transportation to the hotel they've booked in Dublin.

"Should we just get a cab?" Jennifer eyes the long rental car line.

"We may need a car, but it's most likely not going to come back whole, so I'd rather not have a rental agreement with Lincoln and Beth's names on it."

"I could glamour them."

"I think they photocopy the ID. It's not worth the risk. Let's head to long term parking and wait for someone to leave their car. By the time they get back from wherever they're going, we should be back in Pittsburgh." Eddie picks up the heaviest of Jennifer's bags and follows the signs to the long-term lot. They wait around, trying not to arouse suspicion, until a couple leaves a Hyundai Tucson, each dragging two large suitcases.

"They should be gone for awhile," Eddie watches as they enter the terminal before, making his way to the car.

"It's no Ferrari, but I guess this will do." Jennifer wrinkles her nose playfully while she climbs into the passenger seat. Somehow, Eddie unlocks the car and starts the engine. "What hotel did Lincoln book us, anyway?"

"Russell something or other. There's an email confirmation he forwarded me on my phone. Pull up my email and check the address." Eddie begins to laugh.

Jennifer raises her eyebrows and waits for an explanation.

"I just realized that this is the first time that I've *really* driven."

"I knew we should have brought Rocko," Jennifer teases. "Just get us there safe. Looks like it's on Harcort Street, just off of R-110."

The hotel is an older building, but well-kept. Lincoln booked the two of them a honeymoon suite, which Eddie plans to take advantage of as much as possible.

The suite is big and open, and contains a king bed surrounded by four large columns, a claw foot tub, and a fully stocked wet bar. It certainly meets their needs, but Lincoln's real reason for booking this particular hotel was because of the nightlife; it's a spot better known for its nightclubs then for its rustic décor. It's just after noon and the courtyard bar is already beginning to fill.

"It's gonna be a long night, my love. Whaddaya say we have a little fun before we get to work?" Eddie grins seductively as he lifts Jennifer off her feet and carries her toward the bed.

Chapter 48

Eddie lies in bed with his muscular arms wrapped tightly around Jennifer's toned, but shapely vampire body. It takes every bit of willpower that he can muster to release her from his embrace, but he knows that they have a job to do. He can sense Jennifer's mounting anxiety over finding her daughter.

"They won't hurt her, my love." His voice is gentle as he watches her pull his t-shirt over her head. He didn't pack many shirts, and he considers asking for this one back, but if he watches her take it off, he may not be able to control his urge to make love to her again.

She notices him looking at the shirt. "Did you need to wear this?" She grins.

"No, no." Eddie shakes his head, runs his fingers through his hair, and bites his lower lip. "You wear it much better than I ever could. I can grab another shirt at one of the souvenir shops if I need one. Plus, I can't wear a t-shirt if we're going clubbing."

Jennifer bursts into laughter.

"What?" Eddie asks sincerely.

"Nothing, sweetie. You go get your *clubbing* attire on and I'll get ready." She chuckles again before she disappears into the suite's bathroom.

Lincoln.

Hey Eddie, how is Dublin?

Haven't seen much besides the bed yet, if you know what I mean, but we're getting ready to start the search now. Everything going okay back there?

Uh kinda, I guess.

What does that mean? What's wrong?

Abby and Beth are at each other's throats all the time. Nothing I can't handle, though.

I wonder why.

That sounded pretty sarcastic, Eddie. What's that supposed to mean?

Come on, man. Beth has no reason to dislike Abby, except for the fact that you like *Abby.*

Why would Beth care who I like? That makes no sense.

Okay. Listen.

I have no choice.

Fair enough, but I'm going to tell you something, and if you ever tell another soul, I will end you... slowly and painfully.

This sounds fun.

The Editor

Beth was only attracted to me, because I'm a more badass version of you.

Eddie, you don't even— I'm lucky Beth even talks to me. She definitely isn't attracted to me anymore.

Anymore? Did you guys? Ohhhh.

Yes, we dated and were serious, before I went and messed it up. I thought I was King Shit back then and I slept with Sara. Beth found out that I cheated, but not with who. So, we broke up, and I began to write shitty stories.

Wow. Dick move, man. Well, anyway, when we were... together... she called me Lincoln. Twice. It was a real mood killer. Wait? Sara, Noel's mom?

Yes.

How long ago?

I don't know. Probably seven or eight years, I guess.

Holy—

What?

I thought it was just some weird coincidence, but it makes sense. The way she looks, her mannerisms, the reason there's no other parent to take her in. You... are Noel's father.

Chapter 49

Before Lincoln can even process what Eddie had suggested, their mental conversation is interrupted.

Hey, man. I gotta go, but we'll talk, um, later. Eddie exhales slowly as Jennifer emerges from the bathroom wearing a short but classy black cocktail dress that flatters her already attractive figure. Her hair is pulled up into a tight bun, which draws more attention to her eyes. Eddie gets lost in them and it's the one place he doesn't mind being lost.

"You look..." Eddie can't complete the sentence. He just stands there, mouth agape, staring into her eyes.

"Thanks, sweetie." Jennifer giggles as she hands him his sports coat. "Usually I have to glamour a guy to get that reaction."

"Sensational," Eddie finally finishes his thought.

They catch nearly everyone's attention as they walk down to the courtyard bar, which is not necessarily their intention. Anonymity would help them in their search for Perry and his crew.

Eddie makes his way to the bar and orders himself a bourbon and a coffee for Jennifer.

"Only an American would order a Kentucky whiskey in Ireland." The bartender eyes him with disdain. "You probably voted for Trump too, didncha?" He smirks sarcastically as he slides the bourbon glass across the bar. "It'll be a minute for the coffee. The large lad at the end of the bar drank me entire pot." He motions at a mountain of a man a few seats away.

Eddie glances at Jennifer who smiles and nods.

"We don't need the coffee." Eddie tosses a twenty on the bar and puts his arm around Jennifer as they turn to walk away.

"He's a vampire, right?" Eddie looks for Jennifer to confirm the mountain's vampirism, which she does with a nod. Eddie leads her to a far corner of the courtyard where they have a good view of the other vampire and of all the exits.

"We'll wait for him to leave and follow him back to the den," Jennifer whispers.

As they watch the vampire sip coffee, they don't notice any other overly suspicious characters in the garden. Eddie makes a quick run through the nightclub at the hotel, but doesn't notice much besides scantily clad teenage girls and a few drunks that are way too old to be hitting on them. He considers interrupting them, but before he can, his cell phone beeps. *At least they'll get some free drinks,* he thinks as he turns away to read the text message. It's from Jennifer.

Get out here! He's using glamour to force feed two blonde co-eds coffee. Pretty sure he plans to drain them soon.

Eddie quickly makes his way back outside to Jennifer. As soon as he reaches her, the man, with a coed on each arm, exits the courtyard into the hotel lobby.

"They were drinking it straight from the pot and spilling it all over their dresses." Jennifer twists her face in agony as a tear rolls down her cheek. "Perfectly good dresses."

"Let's keep him in our sights, but not get too close. We need him to lead us to Perry."

Eddie grabs Jennifer and they follow the three through the streets of Dublin until they finally stop in an alley behind Christ Church Cathedral. The large vampire grabs the taller woman by the neck and lifts her to his mouth. He bites into her neck viciously. The fear is evident in the smaller woman's eyes, yet she remains motionless.

Eddie takes a step toward them, but he feels Jennifer's firm grasp on his arm.

"We can't, Eddie. We need him to take us to Perry."

"We can't just watch them die!" He pulls free from her grip. "Just be ready to chase him. Call me with a location." Eddie gives Jennifer a quick kiss on the cheek before grunting loudly, sprouting his wings, and taking off towards the male vampire.

The grunt catches the vampire's attention. His eyes grow wide with fear and he drops the woman, who falls to the ground with a sickening thud. The vampire turns and runs straight at the cathedral wall. Eddie soars toward him but just as he reaches for the vampire's collar he disappears through the wall, leaving Eddie with nothing but a fist full of fabric.

Eddie turns sharply, limiting his contact with the wall before falling to the ground. He makes his way to his feet and over to Jennifer and the two younger women.

"You okay, sweetie?" Jennifer asks Eddie as she checks for a pulse on the vampire's victim.

"Wha...? Oh yeah. Weird power for such a big guy, though. Do you want to run around the perimeter and wait for him to come out? So, you don't have to be around all of her blood, I mean."

Jennifer becomes aware for the first time that her fangs are out. "No, I'm fine." She inhales deeply and withdraws her fangs. "She, on the other hand, isn't. Her pulse is weak. I'm afraid that she won't make it."

She looks at the girl's friend, then down at the ground. "Plus, the big guy isn't coming out. There's a crypt in there. I should've known it would be where Perry set up shop."

The dying girl's friend starts to sob uncontrollably. "It's... her... her... birth... day," she gets out between sobs. "She never goes out. I... made her," she confesses before breaking down again.

Jennifer looks at Eddie. "I could..."

Eddie tightens his face and shakes his head before turning his attention to the conscious victim. "What's your name, sweetie?"

Jennifer looks up at the sobbing teen as well.

Her crying slows as she attempts to compose herself. "T... T... Taryn."

"Okay, Taryn. What's her name?" Eddie nods to her dying friend.

"Molly," she whispers.

"Does Molly have any family or anyone who'll miss her for the next few days?"

"Her parents both died a few weeks ago in a bank robbery. I was trying to get her mind off it. She's got a gobshite of a boyfriend, but he could stand to miss her."

Jennifer shifts her eyes back to Eddie. This time he gives a reluctant nod.

Jennifer bites her own wrist and fills Molly's mouth with her blood. "I need to get her back to the hotel. Taryn, you're welcome to come. Russell Hotel, Room 104."

"What about him?" Eddie motions toward the wall that the vampire walked through.

"They'll be expecting us to follow him. Perry likely teleported somewhere else by now anyway. If we wait though, they may think that we don't know that their den is located there and come back."

"But Courtney..." Eddie looks back at the building again.

"She's fine. For now, at least. I can feel that she isn't in any immediate danger. I'll meet you back at the room." Jennifer lifts Molly off the ground and disappears quickly down the street.

"Where'd she go?" Taryn gawks at the spot on the street where her best friend laid just a moment before.

"She's, umm, fast," Eddie replies.

Taryn walks towards Eddie and kisses him softly on the cheek. "Thanks." She smiles seductively. "I would've kissed you on the lips, but I see the way the fast lady looks at you."

Eddie clears his throat. "Um, yeah. We're definitely fond of one another. No problem, though. Can I walk you home?"

"I think I'll join you guys." She smiles again. "I think Molly should see a familiar face when she wakes up."

Eddie shakes his head as he begins the walk back to the hotel. "So, you said her parents died in a bank robbery?"

Chapter 50

Lincoln attempts to drink himself through the flights to Turks and Caicos. There were no first class flights available and in an attempt to avoid any jealousy, he had suggested that Abby and Beth sit together to try to work out their differences.

Neither of them speak a word to each other on either flight.

What's even more uncomfortable is Noel's comfort level with *him*. If she isn't talking to him like a long lost best friend, she's sleeping propped up against him like it's the most comfortable sleep she's ever had.

How could he have not seen it? It's so obvious now; the eyes, the lips, even the way she sleeps. She's a way better looking female version of him at seven years old. He spends the majority of the trip wondering if Noel knows, but of course she doesn't. If Beth knew then maybe Noel would, too, but Beth *doesn't* know. He wonders if he should bring up the possibility to Noel. About ten minutes prior to the flight landing in Providenciales, he makes up his mind that it would have to wait until all this other drama is resolved. He would love to get to know Noel better; heck, he'd always thought he'd be a father someday, anyway. It's just happening differently than he'd imagined.

Maybe it's the copious amount of alcohol that he's consumed, but he actually smiles as he squeezes his daughter gently to wake her. Then he glances to his left, where the beautiful vampire, who he thinks he's falling for, and the gorgeous bartender, who he knows he's always loved, sit. If only he could order another drink.

Chapter 51

Thankfully the ride from the airport to the resort is short, because it is anything but comfortable. The resort sends a van to pick them up but another family going to the same resort arrived late, so they squeeze them into the same van. Lincoln has to cram himself between Beth and Abby, which at one point would have been the start of an incredible fantasy. Right now, it's anything but a dream.

Noel sits in his lap and she is the only one of the four to speak a word on the ride to the resort. Her excitement is contagious, though. She makes friends with the other family and almost makes Lincoln forget that this wasn't just a normal vacation. Both Beth and Abby even crack a grin at one point.

The view as they arrive at the resort is breathtaking. After being greeted with the day's signature drink (and a smoothie for Noel) and unloading their bags in the lobby, they take a tour of the grounds. The resort is divided into four villages, each with its own pool or pools, and each with multiple restaurants. They will be staying in the *Keys Village* section of the resort in a two bedroom suite. Beth and Noel will get one room and Abby will get the other. Originally, Lincoln had hoped to stay with Abby, but now he will gladly sleep on the sofa bed.

Once they get settled into their rooms, they go out and grab a few brick oven pizzas and take them to one of the larger pools to eat. Noel eats one piece and then heads directly to the pool, where she easily assimilates into a group of young children who are swimming relay races. An odd sense of pride swells inside of Lincoln as he watches how easily Noel adapts to different situations— not that he has a real reason to feel responsible for it.

The awkwardness between Beth and Abby quickly intensifies without Noel there as the buffer, and Lincoln begins to plan his escape. He pulls his tacky, flowered shirt back over his pale, but surprisingly trim torso.

"I think I'll head down to the beach to, umm... look for any signs of the ghost pirates."

"I thought you said they only come out at night." Beth glances up from her book. "Why don't you sit down and work on your tan a little bit." She pats her chair, motioning for Lincoln to sit, before spraying her well-toned legs with oil and slowly rubbing it over every inch of them.

The Editor

Lincoln can't help but stare at the legs that he had once known so well. "Come on, I brought some stronger stuff I can put on you. I think you're paler than Abby."

Abby drops her sunglasses to the bridge of her nose and closes her eyes as if concentrating on something. Suddenly a single cloud appears, blocking any direct sun to the pool.

"Come on, Lincoln. I'll go with you. We may be able to find clues as to where they're docking and entering the island, at least. Maybe by the time we get back, the sun will be back out. I'm sure I'll have tired you out by then, so you'll enjoy lounging more." Abby removes her pool cover-up and strolls casually towards the beach, catching nearly every man's attention along the way. Her black and gold swimsuit covers a minimal amount of her pale, but flawless skin.

"Bitch," Beth mumbles as Abby walks away. "Well, go ahead and go." She shoos Lincoln along.

"Beth, I... I mean, do you—"

"Just go. We can talk later. You're right for now, though. You came here to stop the ghost pirates so you need to find out as much about them as possible before tonight. Just plan on a talk later. There are a few things that I need to know."

Lincoln's stomach turns nervously, but he nods and smiles. "I'll always have time for you, Beth." He places a hand on her shoulder for a brief moment before turning and starting to head toward the beach.

"Oh, and Lincoln..."

Lincoln turns around and finds Beth standing directly in front of him. She presses her body against his as she stares up into his eyes and brings his head down to hers until their lips meet. "I haven't forgotten how much fun we used to have."

Chapter 52

The walk back to the hotel drags on and on like a foreign film with no subtitles. It has begun to rain and Taryn could *never* be mistaken for a speed walker. Eddie notices the goose-bumps on her arms and considers wrapping his arm around her but decides against it given their conversation a few minutes ago. He doesn't want to give her any wrong ideas.

"Yeah, so, Molly's parents were depositing some money into Molly's account so that she could pay for her next term at University when this guy and girl come in and rob the place. Molly's dad used to be Garda so he tried to calm them down, and apparently they shot him without a second thought. Then I guess they killed her mum 'cause she wouldn't stop crying. What kind of terrible creature would do such a thing? Probably grew up with no mum or dad. Doesn't take a psychology major like myself to deduce such a thing."

"If you only knew," Eddie replies under his breath.

"What was that?" Taryn uses the opportunity to move closer to Eddie.

Thankfully they've arrived back at the hotel so Eddie gestures toward the door. "After you."

Chapter 53

Lincoln catches up to Abby about a hundred yards down the shoreline, near the end of the resort's property.

"We're not soulmates," she blurts out, catching Lincoln by surprise. "I mean, we didn't imprint or anything. I think you're cute and I can tell by the way you look at me that you wouldn't mind things getting... physical."

Lincoln's face, which was already flushed from the sun and the jog to catch up to Abby, turns crimson.

"And I'd like that, too. It could happen tonight and I'd be happy."

Lincoln, who hasn't been with a woman in nearly two years, now has two women basically offering him intimacy. He notices the sweat that has begun to bead on Abby's chest, the toned muscles of her abdomen, the way her hip bones poke out above her bikini bottoms. He adjusts his swim trunks and tries to think of something clever to say, but before he can speak, Abby continues.

She keeps walking, looking straight ahead, as if in a world of her own. "But what's the point? It doesn't matter how in love with each other we are. I could accidentally bump into someone on a subway, imprint on them, and leave you— no matter how hard it may be to do so." She finally glances at him for a brief second.

A disappointed "Oh," is all Lincoln can muster.

"Beth loves you and I don't want to fight with her. When we get back, I'll tell her that I want to be friends and that you two should be together. Then maybe you guys can enjoy paradise as a couple." She blinks away a tear and forces a smile. "At least until the ghost pirates get here."

"Umm. Yeah, okay, I guess. Let's just see what we can find out about the ghost pirates."

Chapter 54

"So, you're vampires, right?" Taryn uses a towel to dry her damp hair before brazenly removing her barely-wet clothing and sliding into a robe that she finds in the bathroom closet.

Eddie shrugs and shakes his head as Jennifer prepares to answer.

"I am." Jennifer turns to the younger woman and flashes her fangs in mock anger.

Taryn is either oblivious or just pretends not to notice and comes to sit on the bed next to Molly and Jennifer. "So, don't you have to bury her or something?"

"Can't you just mind control her to stop talking or something?" Eddie smirks, only half kidding.

"No need for mind control," Taryn says. "I'll do anything. Anything you guys want me to."

Jennifer laughs. "Okay then, go downstairs and drink three cups of coffee. It's going to be a long night." She licks her lips slowly and winks.

Taryn giggles gleefully and heads down to the lobby in search of coffee. Eddie shoots Jennifer a look once the door closes.

"What? I'm starving. I'm not going to kill her. Now hurry up and meet me in the shower before she gets back. We don't have that long."

"I don't think it'll be a problem." Eddie grins as he watches Jennifer drop her robe.

Chapter 55

As they walk along the shore the hotels and fancy beach homes disappear, and the terrain gets a bit rockier. Eventually they get to a point where they have to climb a fifty-foot rock wall if they want to continue. Abby scales the wall without difficulty and Lincoln is about half way up when she calls down.

"There's a little house up here. They can see everything. I'm gonna knock."

"Wait for me!" Lincoln yells, missing a foothold and barely hanging on until he can regain control of his climb.

"Hurry up, then," she calls back down, annoyed.

Lincoln finally reaches the top and after catching his breath, walks over to meet Abby at the door of the house, which would be more accurately described as a shack.

"Well, what are you waiting for?" Abby shoves Lincoln forward and he readies his hand to knock.

"Come in, Lincoln," a pleasant feminine voice comes from inside.

Chapter 56

"I had four cups!" Taryn calls out as she flings open the bathroom door.

"Whoa! What the...?" Eddie turns around quickly to shield himself from her view.

"Not bad, but I enjoyed the front view better." Taryn laughs confidently. "That tattoo and those abs... you're a lucky woman, Jenny. I got espressos and put ice in them so that I could drink them faster." She stands there like a student awaiting her teacher's approval.

Jennifer, who is every bit as confident, slides open the glass shower doors and hands Eddie a towel before slowly grabbing her own.

"Listen sweetie, I think I may have given you the wrong idea." She strides over to the young woman with the graceful danger of a panther.

"So, we aren't going to... have fun?" Taryn sounds immensely disappointed.

"Oh, sweetie. I'm going to have fun. Eddie will likely have some more fun. But I *do not* share my man."

Nervous tears begin to swell in Taryn's eyes.

The Editor

"Don't worry sweetie, you won't remember anything unpleasant. Eddie turns away as Jennifer sinks her fangs deep into Taryn's neck.

Chapter 57

Lincoln slowly and carefully opens the door as Abby prepares herself for whatever battle may ensue.

"Ease your worries, my friends. I mean you no harm." The high-pitched voice is actually that of a man. He's portly, with a neatly trimmed beard, and looks innocent enough, but Lincoln and Abby remain on guard.

"How do you know my name?" Lincoln asks, sounding more nervous than he would have liked. He stares at the man and while he waits for a response notices the man's eyes change from green to gold in an almost wavelike fashion.

"I know a great deal of things. Please, take a seat. Abby, please join Lincoln." He motions toward two chairs that appear to have been set up in anticipation of their arrival. "Can I get either of you something to eat or drink?"

Abby and Lincoln look around the barren shack and wonder what this man could possibly have to offer them.

"This is weird, Lincoln. We should go." Abby places a hand on his shoulder and pulls him back toward the door.

"Weirder than a vampire who controls the weather and only likes caffeinated blood?" The man laughs heartily.

"He has a point there." Lincoln pulls free from Abby and makes his way to one of the chairs. Abby reluctantly joins him.

"So, you know all about us. How about you tell us your name and how you know these things?" Lincoln tries to sound calm, but his voice still trembles.

"My name is Jophiel. It's not how or what I know that should concern you as much as what I can share with you." Suddenly he reaches out and grabs Lincoln by both sides of his head. The shack is filled with a blinding light.

Abby curls into the fetal position against the closest wall. When she opens her eyes, Lincoln remains in the chair, but stares straight ahead, unblinking, deep in contemplation.

"Lincoln, where did he go?"

No answer.

"Lincoln!" She shakes him to wake him from his trance.

"Wha...? Who?"

"Jophiel! Where is he?"
"Oh. He went back to Heaven, of course."

Chapter 58

"Okay, love, that's enough," Eddie forcibly removes Jennifer from Taryn's neck.

"Good God, her blood is caffeinated to perfection! That was better than an orgasm... no offense, sweetie." Jennifer licks her lips, making sure to savor every last drop. "Lay her down next to Molly. She'll be hungry when she wakes up."

"Yeah, 'cause I'm sure eating her best friend will be just what Molly needs to get over her parents' deaths." Eddie cocks his head to the side and crosses his arms.

"Whatever, just get her out of here. That blood made me so horny!" She throws her towel at Eddie and takes a step toward him. "Let's see if you can make me change my mind on that whole *blood is better than an orgasm* statement."

Normally Eddie would be hopeless against her advances, but the fact that he needs to talk to her about their mission, combined with the nausea from watching her drink Taryn's blood, has given him enough strength to hold out temporarily.

"Wait. Just... give..." He tries to formulate a sentence between her kisses. "Jennifer, hang on. Adam and Evil killed Molly's parents. Perry may have found them already. We need to make a plan and get into that crypt sooner rather than later."

Jennifer pauses. "Okay, but we can't leave Molly to wake up without me. Plus, even though sunlight doesn't kill us, vampires are still creatures of the night and typically sleep more during the day, so tomorrow morning may be a better option for our attack. I can't think straight when I'm this horny and I doubt three minutes will make or break our plan, so get over here."

Chapter 59

"Lincoln, what just happened?" Abby asks, trying not to sound impatient.

Lincoln stares into nothingness for a full minute before finally responding. "Enlightenment."

Abby presses her palm against her forehead as Lincoln slowly gets to his feet.

He turns to the door. "Let's head back. I'll explain everything."

Before she knows it, Lincoln is outside the shack and climbing down the rock wall. Abby leaps from the top of the wall and lands gracefully at the bottom, catching up to him without issue.

"So," Abby spreads her arms, waiting for Lincoln to explain.

Lincoln smiles. "It's all really exciting."

"What is?! Come on Lincoln, snap out of it!"

"We were chosen." Lincoln's voice is soft and he pauses to gaze out at the ocean.

"By?"

"By God, Abby." Lincoln's tone is matter-of-fact.

Abby grabs him by the shoulder and turns him to face her. "I know something weird happened back there, but *what* is going on?"

Lincoln closes his eyes. "Okay. Let me explain. When Jophiel touched my head, I began to see things. Many things; some which I can explain, and some which didn't make any sense at all. How long was I out?"

Abby shakes her head. "I don't know. Maybe thirty seconds?"

Lincoln bursts into laughter. "Unreal. I thought it was days."

"Well, can you tell me some of the things that *did* make sense?"

Lincoln nods. "Jophiel was sent by God to enlighten us. Somehow Lucifer used my laptop as a tool of evil, allowing any evil characters to enter our world to do his deeds."

"But Jennifer and Courtney... they don't seem evil."

"Right. Because God knew what was happening and allowed a balance of good to come in and counteract the evil. Jennifer, Courtney, and then *He* guided me to make Eddie."

Abby stares at Lincoln, not sure what to make of his revelation.

"And the ghost pirates are not working with Perry yet, but they are very much evil and are planning to attack Grace Bay tonight. We need to get back and make sure that Beth and Noel are out of harm's way before we plan our defense."

"We aren't going to defend. We're going to attack," Abby snarls as she glares out into the ocean.

Chapter 60

"Jennifer, shut her up!" Eddie stares at the door nervously, expecting security to burst in at any moment.

The blood-curdling scream would have woken half of the hotel, had anyone been sleeping. In truth, the party downstairs is so loud that no one outside their room likely heard anything at all. Molly's scream did bring Taryn to as well, and they both look equally confused.

Molly scrambles back against the head of the bed. "Taryn? Where...? Who?"

Taryn rubs the sleep from her eyes. "It's okay, they're our friends... I think."

Jennifer slowly approaches the bed and sits near Molly. "That's almost right, but we're more than friends to you Molly. We're family."

Taryn winces at the perceived slight, but tries to be brave for her friend. "Jennifer is a vampire. You were hurt very badly and she saved you. It was the only way."

Molly's eyes widen. "So, I'm a..."

"Vampire," the other three say in unison.

Molly begins to sob. Jennifer embraces her and they remain interlocked until she is calm enough to continue.

"It's not really that bad, dear. I'll help you learn how to survive without killing." Jennifer pulls her closer and calmly strokes her hair.

"And you can feed off of me," Taryn offers kindly.

"Taryn, I don't mean to be rude, but you have served your purpose. It'll probably be best if you head home now." Jennifer's voice remains calm, but it lacks the motherly compassion that she showed Molly.

"No!" Molly shouts. "She is *my* family. So, if I'm *your* family, which I can somehow feel that I am, then so is she." There is a finality in her tone that Jennifer knows not to argue with. "And who in the feck is the creeper in the corner?"

Eddie looks up, confused.

Jennifer stifles a laugh. "That's your fath—That's Eddie. My soulmate. Now, Taryn, be a dear and go get yourself another couple espressos so that Molly can eat."

"No feckin' way! I'm a vegetarian. I can't drink me best friend's blood!" Tears begin to well up in her eyes again.

"Molly, I know that you feel the urge, and it will only get stronger. Trust me. It's easier to feed off of someone that you care about. It's easier to... stop." Jennifer glances at Taryn.

"Glad to see how much I mean to you." Taryn smirks, remembering Eddie having to pry Jennifer off her neck before she passed out. "It's really okay, Molly. It actually feels kinda nice. I'll be right back. I'll see if they have some carrots or something down there too... you know, for old time's sake."

Molly laughs meekly as Taryn springs off the bed.

Eddie shrugs at Jennifer "Girl's got spunk."

Taryn winks at him before turning back to Molly. "I'll do anything for my friends." She turns and skips out the door, headed back down to the lobby bar with a smile on her face.

Eddie pours himself a glass of bourbon. "Okay, so can we figure out how we're going to catch Adam, Evil, Perry and whoever the hell else is out there now?"

"Who are they?" Molly stares at Eddie quizzically. Jennifer shoots Eddie a look.

Eddie shrugs and continues. "Perry is your psychopath grandfather that disowned your mother and wants to take over the world. Adam and Evil are—"

"Eddie, she isn't ready to hear about all of this yet," Jennifer interrupts.

Eddie rolls his eyes. "Anyway. We need to destroy them all before they hurt any more innocent people. So, if you can give Jenny and me a few minutes to plan, I would greatly appreciate it."

"Whatever. Feck off then. I'm still knackered anyway. Just hand me the remote for the tele would ya, ma? I mean, Jennifer."

Jennifer smiles and turns on the television for Molly before handing her the remote and taking a seat by Eddie at the table.

"Well, where do we start?" She turns to Eddie hoping, and knowing, that he has an answer.

Before he can speak, something on the TV catches Molly's attention. "Hey, looks like your chancers are out acting the maggot again."

Eddie and Jennifer look at each other and shrug. "Sweetie, we're going to need you to cut down on the slang a bit so us *whankers*, I believe it is, can understand you." Jennifer grins.

Molly chuckles. "Your *Adam and Evil*," she points to the screen. "Looks like they robbed another ban—"

Chapter 61

"Where have you guys been? It's so much fun here!" Noel shrieks as she runs up and gives Lincoln a giant hug.

Lincoln hugs Noel back and smiles at Beth, who is glowing from her time in the sun. "I'm glad you're having a good time, sweetie. Go swim a little more before we have to head back to the room." He grins at Noel, who is back in the pool before he can even finish the sentence. "Beth, we need to talk." He smiles shyly.

"But first, *we* need to talk." Abby steps between Lincoln and Beth, who just rolls her eyes.

"I'd like nothing more," Beth mumbles.

Lincoln walks away to watch Noel swim, and Abby sits down on a lounge chair next to Beth and takes a deep breath. "Look, I know there has been some tension between us. We both have feelings for Lincoln."

Beth starts to deny it, but Abby just continues. "You're better for him, plain and simple. I would eventually hurt him, because of what I am. We're not imprinted on each other. You and he should try to be together. It'll be good for Noel if it works out, too. She's really taken to him."

Beth sits there in stunned silence for a full minute. "I wasn't expecting any of that. Thank you," she says, extending a hand to Abby. Abby smiles and takes her hand.

The moment their skin touches, each is met with an almost indescribable feeling. Intensely hot but at the same time pleasantly cool. Numb but at the same time every nerve ending explodes with ecstasy. They see everything, yet only each other. The normal sounds of the resort pool sound like an angelic symphony.

Startled, they release their grip, although they both regret doing so.

Lincoln is making his way toward them as they try to regain their composure. "So, is everything okay with two of my three favorite ladies, now?" He knows how cheesy it sounds, but says it anyway.

Beth avoids eye contact with Lincoln. "Um..."

"Yes, we're all good now." Abby grabs Lincoln by the arm. "Let's get Noel and head back to talk about what Jophiel showed you."

"But wait. I wanted to—" Lincoln pulls his arm free, wanting to have his conversation with Beth.

"Who's Jophiel?" Beth asks quickly; mainly out of curiosity, but also to avoid Lincoln's conversation.

Chapter 62

"Molly, get a grip, sweetie." Jennifer speaks calmly, as if speaking to an unruly child, while physically restraining the new vampire so that she doesn't smash the television. Eddie begins to walk closer to help Jennifer, but she waves him off. "Don't, Eddie. She can't control her emotions right now. She won't hurt me because of our bond, but she'll try to rip out your throat without a second thought."

Eddie smirks. "Well, tell her I'm about to be her new daddy so she better get those emotions under control because I'm not going anywhere."

"Just go down and stall Taryn for a few minutes until I can get Molly under control. She'll never forgive me if I let her kill her best friend."

Eddie nods and leaves the room. Molly begins to shake uncontrollably and then breaks down in Jennifer's arms. "I miss them, Mom," Molly sobs. Jennifer dons a look of concern, but lights up inside at hearing Molly call her mom.

"I know, sweetie. But we *will* avenge them."

"But how? I couldn't hurt you even if *you* had killed them. Isn't Perry your father?" Molly's eyes resemble those of a curious toddler, which is fitting, since that's basically what she is in the vampire world.

"Perry released me from that obligation." Jennifer's tone is cold and she stares out the window searching for what to say next.

"Well, I want to be there." Molly sits up tall, mustering all the strength that she can to stop crying and to try to sound brave.

"That is out of the question, sweetie." Jennifer meets Molly's big brown eyes with a stare that Molly doesn't dare question. "It's much too dangerous for even the most skilled vampire. You haven't even had a chance to cultivate a special power yet."

"A special power? I'm an immortal vampire. How much more special does it get?"

"Plenty," is all that Jennifer replies, signaling that any further questions on the subject would be answered at a later time. "Eddie and Taryn are on their way back. Do you think you're in control enough now to feed on Taryn without killing her? She's probably still weak from... never mind, you just can't drink too much."

"I'm fine, Mom." Molly takes a deep breath and holds it for a few seconds.

"Good, because I really have to pee." Jennifer uses every bit of her speed to get into the bathroom.

Molly hears Taryn's voice in the hallway and takes another deep breath and grips the sheets of the bed tightly.

Eddie enters the room slowly with Taryn following close behind. "Jenny, are we clear?" He asks, scanning the room searching for Jennifer, then grinning at Molly, who just rolls her eyes in return.

"Yes, yes. I'll be right out," she calls out from the bathroom.

"You won't believe what Lincoln just told me." Eddie drops some ice from the ice bucket into a glass and pours himself some more bourbon. He hears a sigh behind him and turns around. Taryn's robe drops to the ground and Molly has her fangs buried deep into her femoral artery.

"Oh geez," Jennifer frowns as she emerges from the bathroom. She smacks Eddie in the back of the head. "Don't just stand there staring!" She quickly makes her way to the bed to separate the best friends.

"Uhh, sorry, love. Just caught me a little by surprise, I guess." Eddie grins and shrugs as he takes another swallow of the bourbon.

Jennifer rolls her eyes when she is finally able to separate the two.

"That was incredible!" Taryn gasps, trying to catch her breath.

"Glad you had fun. Thirty more seconds and you'd have been dead," Jennifer scolds the two. "Molly, that should be enough blood to hold you over until we can get back to the states."

"The states? I'm not leaving Dublin," she begins to protest, but after a glare from Jennifer, she closes her mouth slowly, resigned to the fact that she will be leaving sooner rather than later.

"Can we at least bring Taryn, then? I don't want to have to deal with all the U.S. whankers on me own."

"We'll see. Right now, Eddie and I have more important things to figure out."

Chapter 63

Lincoln is in an almost manic state when they get back to the condo. Abby excuses herself to take a shower and give Lincoln some time to discuss what happened with Jophiel to Beth, amongst other things.

They order Noel a pizza from the resort brick oven pizza shop and set her up in the living room, watching some sort of show that little kids watch on some sort of little kids' TV station. Lincoln realizes that he has a lot to learn about having a daughter, but is giddy about doing so. He kisses Noel softly on the head before heading into the bedroom where Beth is waiting for him.

"Hello, gorgeous," He attempts to kiss Beth's soft lips, but is instead met with her left cheek. "Oh. Um, did I do something? Oh shit. This is about Noel, huh? I just—I didn't know until all of this, and we had more important—"

"What in the hell are you talking about? You didn't know what?" Beth looks genuinely shocked and confused.

The Editor

"Look, Beth. I was stupid. I'm sorry for being stupid, but I'm not sorry that Noel came about because of my stupidity."

Beth's eyes narrow for a few moments before springing open wide. "Oh, you've got to be shitting me! You didn't... my sister? You asshole!"

Before Lincoln can respond, Beth's fist slams against the side of his eye and the next thing he feels is the cold hard tile against the other side of his face. The commotion attracts Noel's attention and she comes in from the living room. Abby bursts in from the other bedroom wrapped in a towel.

Abby tries to stop her, but Beth pushes past them all. Lincoln jumps as the condo door slams, but motions that he's okay and for Abby to get dressed and go find Beth.

"Lincoln, what happened?" Noel asks as she sits down next to him on the bedroom floor.

Lincoln sits quietly for a moment, as he ponders the best way to respond. "Noel, grownups are sometimes... No—*most* of the time we're not as good as kids like you. A while ago, I made a mistake that hurt your Aunt Beth. She just found out more about that mistake, and now she needs some time to process it. I've lived with that mistake bottled up inside me for a long time and I should *not* have done that. The thing is, I probably would've kept it inside forever, except for the fact that I found out something beautiful had come from my actions. That something beautiful... is you."

Noel stares at Lincoln with pizza sauce on her chin, trying to make sense of his rambling.

"So what mistake did I make, Lincoln? I'm sorry," she whispers as tears begin to form in her big brown eyes.

Lincoln grabs Noel and pulls her tight against his chest. "No, no, no, baby doll. You haven't made a mistake since I've met you. What I am trying to tell you is that I found out that I'm your father."

Noel smiles at Lincoln but shakes her head. "Lincoln, I would like it if you *were* my daddy, but my mama said that she didn't know who my daddy was and she knew you at least a little."

Lincoln laughs at the irony of her innocent statement.

"Yes, that's what your mama told everyone, but I think that she said that because she didn't want to hurt your Aunt Beth's feelings. That's all grown up stuff, though. The important thing is that I'm your dad. We can take a test to prove it when we get back to Pittsburgh. And no matter what that test says, I'll always be there for anything that you need. Okay, baby doll?"

The Editor

Noel smiles from ear to ear and nestles in close to Lincoln. "Okay, Papa."

Chapter 64

"So, should we go after Adam and Evil first, or hit Perry's lair and hope everyone is there?" Jennifer asks, trying to speak softly; it's evident Molly is listening in.

"We already know where the lair is. If we hit it, save Courtney, kill Perry, Lisa, and whoever else we can, then our trip is a success. We don't even know if they've met Adam and Evil yet," Eddie replies at a normal volume.

Jennifer notices Molly glare at Eddie out of the corner of her eye. "Regardless of whether they've met or not, Adam and Evil still need to be dealt with." She glares at Eddie while nodding her head in Molly's direction. Molly sits on the bed with her jaw clenched and nostrils flared, still pretending to watch the television.

Eddie nods. "Understood, but we hit the lair today after the last tour. Perry should be gathering the troops to hand out the night's orders at that time. The civilians in the church will be minimal." Eddie glances at Molly, then shifts his eyes back to meet Jennifer's.

Jennifer nods in agreement before Eddie speaks again. "And *they* stay here."

"Of course." Jennifer agrees, holding up a hand to silence the protest that was about to come from the eavesdropping Molly's mouth. "Taryn, go home. Gather what you want to take. We'll be leaving for the U.S. shortly."

Taryn opens her mouth, but no sound escapes it.

"Will that be a problem?" Jennifer snaps.

"No ma'am." Taryn speaks softly, as she slips her clothes from the night before back on and waves to Molly as she heads out the door.

"Molly, you are to wait here. Contact us if anything comes up at all. I left my cell number on the nightstand next to the bed. *We*," Jenifer points back and forth between herself and Eddie, "will handle Adam and Evil, but there are other dangers that require our attention as well, so we need to be ready to go at a moment's notice. Do you have a passport?"

Molly shakes her head.

"Never mind. Nothing a little glamour won't fix, I suppose. I'll teach you when we get back. Just *DO NOT LEAVE* this room. Understand?"

Molly begrudgingly nods, but the defiance in her eyes is evident.

"Molly, it's important. These people are danger-ous, and you are... well, young. Eventually you'll be able to help us, but now isn't the time. I promise you that I'll give Adam and Evil everything that they deserve. Can you just trust me on that?" Eddie tries his best to sound sympathetic.

Molly's eyes soften some, but she doesn't speak. Instead, she gives another solemn nod and changes the channel on the television.

Eddie takes another gulp of bourbon and follows Jennifer out of the room. "Good Lord, she's going to be impossible."

Jennifer laughs. "All new vampires are like that. The new bloodlust is worse than any hormone-fueled rage that human teenagers get." She pauses. "At least I guess it is. Technically, I was never a human teenager, but that's how Lincoln wrote it." She laughs.

Eddie shakes his head. "This is all bat-shit crazy." He grins. "See what I did there. You're a vampire. *Bat* shit crazy."

Jennifer rolls her eyes. "Really, Eddie? You're better than that. That's something lame that Lincoln would say. Plus, vampires—"

"Don't really turn into bats. I know, I know."

Chapter 65

Abby has never been so happy to be a vampire. She's able to dress and catch Beth before she even makes it down the stairs from their third floor condo. "Beth, wait!" Abby reaches out and catches her by the arm.

The fireworks explode again and Beth almost forgets why she's mad. "Let go, Abby." She tries hard to sound like she means it.

"Listen, Beth. I know it may feel weird that Lincoln is your niece's father, but that's a good thing. You can tell she really wants a father, and with us imprinting she wasn't going to get one. The fact that Lincoln is her father is great! We can all still be close. As close as you want." She says with a wink. "It's not like he is going to turn all this down." She motions to herself and Beth.

"I *want* to cut it off," Beth hisses and Abby bursts into laughter. "It's not funny, Abby! He screwed my sister while we were together."

"Oh." Abby stops laughing quickly. "I didn't real-ize..." She pauses thoughtfully before wiping a tear from Beth's high cheekbone and kissing her softly on her puffy pink lips. "It was a long time ago, hun. We have all changed a lot since then—some more than others." She smirks and gestures at herself. "Why don't we go back to the condo and sort this out? We really have some other important things to talk about as well. As far as all of this goes, Lincoln cares for you deeply, I've known that from the first time I saw him look at you. I knew that if he ever had to choose, he would choose you, and that's why I made the excuse about my imprinting. How funny is it that *we* imprinted?" She chuckles, shaking her head.

"I doubt Lincoln will find it that funny," Beth replies softly.

"He wanted us to get along. He needs to worry about learning how to be a father now, anyway. Having two beautiful women there to help him can't hurt," Abby takes Beth by the hand and leads her back up the steps to the condo. "Come on. You have to hear what happened to us while we were gone."

Chapter 66

Eddie and Jennifer decide on a restaurant between Castle and Fishamble streets to kill time before their attack. It's a busy, upscale bar where they can remain unnoticed, and it's close enough to Christ Church that they can monitor anything unusual that may happen while they're waiting. The hostess shows them to a booth in the back, but is happy to seat them in an open booth with a window view once Jennifer *asks* her to.

Eddie takes in the dark décor as he sips his Blanton's and thinks about how this is his kind of place. Jennifer sips a cappuccino and stares out the window nervously.

"It will be fine, love." Eddie tries to reassure her. "I told you what the angel, or whatever, told Lincoln. *God* basically made us to defeat Perry and his army." He takes her cold, but soft hand in his.

"I know. But I still worry about *her*. What if they..." She stops, starting to tear up.

"Don't think like that, Jenny. Lisa and Courtney were together for so long. That has to count for something, doesn't it?"

"I hope so," she whispers before going back to staring out the window.

They wait at the bar until just before 5:15, when they get up and head to Christ Church. Admittance stops at 5:15 but Jennifer can glamour their way inside as long as there is someone to glamour. The last tour should finish up around six, so they plan to wait for that tour to finish before making their way down to the crypt.

When they arrive at the entrance to Christ Church they're surprised to see a line of people, most wearing large fur coats, waiting to be admitted to the facility. They get to the door just as the last of the line has been admitted and are met by a small man with bright red hair who is smiling ear to ear.

"Top of the evening to ya."

Jennifer bursts into laughter.

Eddie shoots her a confused glance, but the man pays her no attention. "You folks here for the Cat and Mouse party?" he asks, not waiting for an answer. "Two hundred U.S.," he says, holding out his hand.

"Are ye gonna stick it in ye pot of gold?" Jennifer mumbles under her breath, laughing again until she catches an elbow from Eddie.

"No problem, sir." Eddie hands him the money.

"Down the stairs to the crypt. No flash photography with the cat and mouse." He motions for them to enter.

"What is *wrong* with you?" Eddie laughs as they make their way to the staircase that leads down to the crypt.

"That was the most stereotypical leprechaun I have ever seen!" Jennifer bursts into an almost uncontrollable laughter again.

Eddie shakes his head disapprovingly. "Okay, get it together. I don't know what a cat and mouse party is, but I don't want to be the mouse." He rounds a corner and bumps into a woman who's wearing nothing but cat ears, a tail, and some painted-on whiskers.

"That's a pity." The woman smiles at Eddie before looking Jennifer up and down, as if sizing up her competition. "I would've thoroughly enjoyed a game of cat and mouse with you." She purrs and runs a finger seductively over Eddie's chest.

Jennifer hisses at the woman and slaps her hand away from Eddie's chest.

"Easy, girly. If you're the mouse of the couple, I'm definitely not a cat you want to tangle with." The woman stands up a little taller, proudly displaying her curvy physique before turning and walking down a long hallway.

Eddie smirks as he watches Jennifer's reaction. "Well, she felt warm, so I

don't—"

"She was human," Jennifer hisses. Eddie laughs harder this time.

Eddie motions down the hallway. "We're walking into a crypt that likely houses a den of vampires. There's only one way in and out. Once we're in we'll have to fight our way back out so I need you to be alert. So, calm it down a bit before we go any further, okay?"

Jennifer takes a deep breath and grins. "Cool as a vampire." She winks.

Chapter 67

The energy in the condo is uneasy, but everyone is being polite and Noel is beaming. Her energy brings a smile to everyone's faces.

"So, Lincoln, you need to explain everything to Beth, but before you do, we need to explain something to you." Abby shuffles her feet nervously.

"I get it, I really do. Beth has every right to be mad at me," he whispers back, trying to avoid Noel's ears, as she has gone back to the other room to draw.

"We imprinted," Beth blurts out, almost sounding boastful.

Lincoln smiles. "I know how right for each other we were... *are*. And I'm truly sorry for how stupid I was, but I don't think we can—."

Abby grimaces. "No, Lincoln. *We* imprinted." She grabs Beth's hand, sending shock waves through both of them.

Lincoln tries to mask his shock but the quiver in his voice betrays him. "Oh. That's... great."

Abby quickly jumps back in. "We don't want to hurt you. In fact, we'd still like to kind of live as a family with you and Noel. If that's okay with you?"

Lincoln gets up from the table and walks around into the adjoining kitchen. "Um... yeah, of course. So, let's talk about Jophiel and how we're going to get Beth and Noel to safety. It's already getting dark."

Lincoln calmly explains as much as he can to Beth over the next twenty minutes, most of which is Beth asking questions and offering logical reasons that Lincoln may have hallucinated all of this. When Abby confirms that something happened, she finally accepts Lincoln's words as truth.

"So, we need to get you and Noel somewhere safe, like, five minutes ago." Lincoln gets up from the table.

Beth looks at Noel and closes her eyes. "Lincoln, we aren't going to be any safer than we are here with you and Abby." She sounds almost reluctant.

"She's right, Lincoln. We can't trust anyone here as much as we can trust ourselves. Didn't you have any *good guys* that may have slipped into this world from the ghost pirates' story?"

Lincoln grimaces. "No. It was a horror story. Like I said, I was in a dark place." He glances at Beth quickly, remembering how he wrote the story shortly after their break-up. "Unless..."

"Unless what?" the women reply in unison.

"Black Jack," Lincoln answers, more to himself than to them.

Abby and Beth wait impatiently for him to explain.

Lincoln begins to pace the condo floor. "He was a poet. They raided his town and captured him early in the novel. The pirates made him part of their crew because he could write, and they wanted him to journal their exploits. He wasn't a hero, but he definitely wasn't a fan of the crew, and he knows everything about them. Maybe if we can get to him, he can tell us how to stop them. Or, at least how to keep them occupied until Eddie gets here."

Abby raises an eyebrow. "So, is he a ghost, too?"

"He wasn't originally, but they tricked him into drinking from *The Seadog's Cup,* which is a relic that they stole. It turned them all into the immortal ghost pirates," Lincoln explains, starting to get excited about telling one of his stories.

Beth shrugs. "Well, I guess it's worth a shot. Any idea how we can separate him from the rest of the crew?"

Lincoln shakes his head and closes his eyes to think.

"I have an idea. What does he look like?" Abby asks.

"What are you going to do?" Concern marks Lincoln's face.

"I'm going to take a Hobie Cat from the watersports area and sail it out close to their ship when it approaches. Then, I'll cause a storm violent enough to capsize their ship and keep them in the water at which point I'll scan the water, find him, and bring him back. Easy-peasy." She shrugs.

Lincoln pinches the bridge of his nose, then nods. "I guess it's as good a plan as any. Can you keep yourself safe?"

Abby snaps her fingers and it begins to rain on Lincoln's head and follows him wherever he moves until he finally stops moving.

Beth bursts into laughter.

Abby winks. "I'm pretty precise with my powers."

"Fair enough," Lincoln grumbles, grabbing a towel from the bathroom and drying himself off. "Black Jack is about two inches taller than me and husky."

"Seriously? That's it? Anything else that might help me find him?" Abby leans forward, elbows on the table.

Lincoln thinks for a minute and grins. "He's also the only black pirate on the ship if that helps. I modeled him after a buddy of mine. Kind of resembles a young Terrence Howard."

The Editor

"Idiot," Abby mumbles under her breath. "Okay, wait here with Beth and Noel. I'll be back with Jack shortly."

Chapter 68

Eddie and Jennifer carefully make their way down the hallway and into the crypt.

"What in the hell?" Eddie's eyes grow wide and he laughs.

An incredibly fit, dark-skinned woman wearing only cat ears and contacts that resemble cat eyes approaches them. "Cat or mouse?" she asks in an accent that's more British than Irish. She tries to remove Eddie's coat.

The room is full of people in some form of either cat or mouse attire. Jennifer giggles when a husky man and woman wearing nothing but the Mickey Mouse ears, like you would get at Disney world stroll by. "That *is* freakin' awesome."

There is no sign of Perry or any vampire from what Eddie can tell.

"Neither," Eddie answers politely.

"What *is* this?" Jennifer is not nearly as politely.

The woman purrs softly before answering. "This is the party to honor the mummified cat and mouse housed here. We of an alternative lifestyle gather here and have some fun. Did you mean to go to the party at the Church of Adam and Eve?"

Eddie raises his eyebrows.

"I may go there next," she flashes a seductive smile. "It's in honor of this *Adam and Evil* that have been all over the news. You dress up as your favorite villain. Supposedly, the host does an awesome Dracula impersonation. I may go as *naked cat woman*." She winks at Eddie before turning and walking away.

"We need to get there, now. It has to be Perry, and throwing a party in Adam and Evil's honor is how he intends to meet them." Jennifer is already making her way back down the hall toward the stairway.

Eddie smirks as he jogs to catch up. "So, who are you going as?"

They hit a second-hand store and a costume shop and show up to the Church of Adam and Eve about an hour and a half later. Jennifer is decked out in a blue pantsuit and a short blonde wig and Eddie wears a black suit with a red trucker hat and some comically large hands that he found at the costume store.

"What if we need an invitation?" Jennifer asks as they approach the church.

"We aren't going in the front door. Follow me," Eddie grabs her hand as he heads down an alley.

They come to an entrance on the rear side of the building and before he can even try the door, it opens, revealing a smiling Priest. He ushers them inside. "Come in, come in. We've been expecting you."

Jennifer shoots Eddie a look. He shrugs. The Priest, seeming to read their minds, laughs. "The Lord will provide."

Eddie reaches into his inside pocket for his flask, but pauses when he notices the Priest staring at him. "Umm...may I?"

"By all means. There are a lot of them down there." The priest gives a sideways nod toward Jennifer while lifting Eddie's hand that holds the flask to his mouth.

Eddie takes a sip and rubs his forehead. "Lead the way, Father."

Chapter 69

With Abby gone, half of the buffer between Beth and Lincoln is also gone, so Beth kisses Noel on the head and heads to her bedroom. She ignores Lincoln, who remains seated next to Noel on the couch watching a kid's show. It's about twin sisters who, although they look the same, are actually quite different.

Just like Beth and Sara. Lincoln thinks.

What, who's Sara? Oh, Sara!

Damnit, Eddie. Get out!

Hey, I'm pretty busy here. You know, saving the world and shit. You're the one who's thinking so hard right now that I can't ignore it. Wait... What?

Lincoln hears Eddie's raucous laughter inside his head.

What's so funny?

Dude, your luck is the worst. Abby and Beth imprinted? *You couldn't have written that better yourself.*

Hardy-har-har, Eddie. How soon can you get here? I'm not sure we can defeat the ghost pirates without you. Abby is working on something, but we could use the help.

I'm trying, man. I have my hands full with some unforeseen developments here.

What kind of developments?

Nothing I can't handle. Let's just say that you aren't the only father in our little group anymore.

Lincoln rubs his head.

I don't think I even want to know. Just get here as soon as you can. Please.

Chapter 70

Abby sneaks down to the now-closed resort watersports shop. After waiting for a young couple to slowly walk by, she scampers down to where the Hobie Cats are located and pushes one into the surf. She can't help but wonder why she, who's deathly afraid of a goldfish, is taking a glorified raft with an attached sail out into an ocean filled with sharks.

She swings the sail out wide, ducking under the arm as it moves to her right. The sail catches wind and she does her best to navigate the raft towards where Jophiel had said the Pirates would be.

A splash of warm salt water hits her in the face as she makes it past the break, but the water is relatively calm after that.

"Freakin' Lincoln," she says to herself but out loud. "Ghost Pirates? Really?" She wipes her face in disgust and sails out much further than she is comfortable with. It's hard to make out in the dark, but it seems that in the distance, a faint glow is beginning to appear. She watches as the glow gets larger and larger, until finally she can make out the sails of *The Bearded Ghost*.

"Showtime." She lifts her hands, commanding waves to strike the starboard side of the ship. She pounds the side of the ship with wind and waves until she begins to hear the cries of the men on board as they fight to remain on deck.

Abby takes a deep breath and summons all the wind that she can. She sends it toward the boat, finally capsizing it. She snaps her fingers and a bolt of lightning strikes the center of the ship, setting it ablaze.

Lincoln had explained to her that no matter what she did to the boat and everyone on it, they would eventually regenerate, but all she needed was enough time to find Black Jack— this should do the trick.

She uses her own wind to expertly navigate the sea from drowning pirate to drowning pirate. Some are scarier than others, but none fit the description that Lincoln provided for Jack.

Finally, after completely circling the boat twice and almost abandoning her mission, she gazes up amidst the flames and what remains of the ship to the silhouette of a man who seems to be sitting and reading. No, writing.

"Jack?!" she calls out desperately. "Jack, is that you?!"

The Editor

The silhouette stands and a face peeks out just above the flames. "Who's asking?"

"Wow, you really do look like a young Terrence Howard."

The pirate stares at her blankly.

"Never mind. Come on! Jump down. I'm getting you outta here." She motions for him to board the raft.

"Um, no offense madam, but I don't know you and I'm not boarding that tiny boat." His voice is deep and velvety.

"Instead you'll sit on the burning remains of a sinking ship?" she replies impatiently.

"Both the ship and I will be back tomorrow evening." He sighs as he sits back down in the flames.

"I don't have time for this." Abby makes a quick looping motion with her hand and then grabs at the air, as if pulling Jack closer to her. A mini tornado lifts Jack out of his boots and carries him toward her.

Jack's eyes are like two full moons as he approaches the raft.

"Can I put you down on the raft or do you need to ride the tornado in to shore?"

Chapter 71

The priest leads them down an ornately decorated hallway lined with golden framed paintings representing the Book of Genesis. At the end of the hallway is what seems to be a reinforced steel door. The priest stops just short of the entryway.

"This is where I bid you adieu, I'm afraid." The priest smiles again, but it's not like the one he greeted them with. This is a nervous smile. "Down the stairway and follow the sound through the halls. You'll come to a ballroom of sorts. That's where the party is." Without waiting for a response, the priest turns and walks back toward where they had met him.

"Um, okay." Jennifer shrugs as she eases open the heavy door. It groans as it slowly swings open, almost as if warning them to stay out. Slowly and quietly they follow the sounds and eventually enter the ballroom, seemingly unnoticed through a back entrance.

Eddie scans the room for any signs of Perry or Adam and Evil. To his left there is a table with large baskets of apples on top and a sign reading *"Take*

One—You Can't Commit the Original Sin Twice, Can You?"

Eddie shakes his head and glances around some more, spotting party goers dressed as every villain imaginable from Judas Iscariot, to Hitler, to The Joker... And Harley Quinns. Lots and *lots* of Harley Quinns.

"They do know there are other female villains, right?" Jennifer rolls her eyes, as if reading his mind.

Eddie laughs and shakes his head. "Apparently not. Any sign of them?"

Before Jennifer can answer, the main lights go dim and strobe lights kick on. A voice booms over a loudspeaker, but the person hidden from their view.

"Good Evening. I vant to thank you all vor coming to this celebration. Our guests of vonor should arrive shortly. Until then, enjoy yourselves. I vill see you soon."

Eddie looks to Jennifer. "Was that...?"

Jennifer nods. "Yes. It was the worst Dracula impression ever." She smirks. "And yes, it was Perry."

She notices something catch Eddie's eye behind her and turns back toward the main entrance. "You *have got* to be freaking kidding me."

Chapter 72

Jack agrees to ride to shore peacefully on the raft with Abby. She sets him down gently and uses the wind to catch her sail, guiding them in smoothly.

Jack opens his mouth, but Abby holds up a hand commanding silence. "Just listen. You are a character from a book, brought to life by forces of evil. I'm Abby, a vampire, created by another evil character brought to life the same way. I chose to join with the good guys who God is assembling to destroy the evil. I'm taking you to meet the author who wrote your story— who also happens to be one of the good guys. Got it?"

Jack opens his mouth but closes it again without speaking. Then he shrugs and grins. "Makes about as much sense as anything else," he says with a smooth English accent. "Do you mind if I write all of this down?"

"Knock yourself out." Abby guides the raft smoothly onto the sand. "Hey, why don't you talk like…"

Jack smirks. "Like a pirate? Sometimes it be slippin' out, here and thur. I'll try to make more of an effort to give you the authentic pirate experience going forward, Madam."

Abby rolls her eyes. "Yeah, you seem like one of Lincoln's creations. Let's go. It's not far." She waves for him to follow as she heads up the beach toward the resort pool area. She stops to rinse her feet at one of the shower stations and waits for Jack to do the same. Jack shrugs and rinses the sand from his glowing feet.

"What? There's nothing worse than getting sand all over your condo and stepping on it after you're clean," Abby snaps.

"I can think of a few worse things," Jack mumbles. "I just think you better get me somewhere more private soon. People generally do not react well to seeing a glowing pirate, in my experience."

"Shit, you're right. Drape this over your head and follow me." She tosses him a towel from one of the poolside stands and takes off in a jog toward the condo. Luckily, they don't pass anyone along the way. When they make it to the condo, Lincoln is waiting up for them with Noel asleep in his lap. The noise of the door opening and closing is loud enough to wake both her and Beth.

Beth can't help but gasp when she opens the bedroom door and comes face to face with a smiling Jack.

"Hello, madam." He greets her kindly.

Lincoln tries to stand between Jack and Noel, in an attempt to shield her from his frightening glow, but she pushes past him as if nothing is out of the normal at all.

"Who's this?" she asks with a curious innocence that only a child could manage.

"Name's Jack." The Pirate extends her a glowing hand. "And who might ye be?"

Noel laughs. "Ye?"

"He wants to know your name." Beth uses her best motherly voice and pulls Noel back away from Jack.

"My name is Noel," she answers, blushing.

"Argh. Princess Noel, a pleasure indeed." He then turns his attention to Lincoln. "And I take it you'd be the writer, then?"

Lincoln nods.

"So, an escape plan was out of the question? Forcing me to watch the things that they did, over and over..."

"He was in a dark place," Abby and Beth say in unison.

Lincoln runs his hands through his hair. "What we need to focus on is stopping those things from happening here. Any ideas on how we can do that?"

Jack sits down at the table. "Besides having Abby do what she did every night for the rest of time? I'm gonna need a fair amount of ye rum while I ponder that one."

Lincoln grabs a bottle and a glass from the kitchen and sets them in front of Jack, who begins to chuckle.

"I haven't had a need for a glass in quite some time."

Chapter 73

Standing in the entrance is Taryn, dressed as what appears to be *Sexy Maleficent*. Behind her is Molly.

"Well, this is a surprise," Eddie says mockingly. "Who's she supposed to be anyway?"

Jennifer's face flashes a moment of pride between angry scowls. "Lady Macbeth, of course."

"Okay, well never mind them right now." Eddie tugs at Jennifer's arm. Jennifer tries to pull away but Eddie won't release the grip. "Jenny, we need to stay out of sight. Perry doesn't know those two, so they're safe. Let's go, we need to plan our attack."

Jennifer finally gives in and follows Eddie into a hallway and up a flight of stairs to a balcony, where they have the advantage of seeing everyone below while being hidden by the cover of darkness.

"How many vampires do you see?" Eddie asks.

"Six at least, but it's hard to tell with some of the costumes."

"Good. I counted six too, plus Perry and Courtney, wherever they are. Lisa, dressed as the iceberg that sunk the Titanic is over in the corner talking to vampire Richard Nixon. Then Kim Jong-un, Ray Lewis— who looks like the guy from last night— Bernie Madoff, and Tonya Harding."

"Oh, I missed Bernie. Seven plus Perry, then. You didn't see Ursula, I guess," she says pointing her out. "Shit..."

"What's the matter?" Eddie raises an eyebrow.

"They can sense her... Molly. And she can sense them. We need to get down there."

Before they can react, Perry appears in the middle of the dance floor below them dressed as Dracula with an unfamiliar vampire beside him dressed as the Bride of Dracula. Below them, kneeling and chained, is Courtney. The entrance draws "oohs" and "ahhs" and a round of applause from the crowd.

"Velcome. I have just been invormed that our guests of vonor have arrived. Place your hands, paws, and tentacles together for Adam and Evil!" The spotlights hit the entrance and Adam and Evil appear hand in hand.

Molly releases a guttural growl and springs forward, striking Adam and ripping off his left arm. Pandemonium ensues giving Jennifer and Eddie the opportunity to strike as well.

Adam laughs as Evil tosses him an apple from the table. He bites into it and before he can even swallow the bite, his arm completely regenerates. Evil circles around behind Molly, who stares at Adam in disbelief.

Jennifer goes straight for Courtney, freeing her from the chains and somewhat evening the odds. Eddie easily removes the heads of vampire Madoff and vampire Tonya Harding before ripping out their hearts and throwing them at the feet of vampire Ray Lewis.

"Shall we finish this?" Eddie grins at the larger man.

Lewis disappears through the wall to his right, then reappears behind Eddie and knocks him to the ground.

As Adam and Evil toy with Molly and Taryn, Jennifer and Courtney try to make their way towards Molly to help, but vampires Ursula and Kim Jong-un stand in their way. Ursula emits a black mist, shielding them from Jennifer and Courtney's view. Suddenly, Courtney begins to choke herself.

"What are you doing?" Jennifer asks, desperately trying to pull Courtney's hands from her own neck.

"It's... his power. He's in... control," she gasps.

"Use yours!" Jennifer shouts.

"Still... weak from... chains," Courtney gasps as tears build up in her eyes.

"You are older and stronger. Now do it," Jennifer commands, refusing to give up. Courtney closes her eyes and focuses. Slowly her hands begin to release their grip and through the smoke emerges Vampire Jong-un.

Jennifer easily removes his head, then heart, and throws it angrily into the smoke. The smoke begins to intensify and soon, Jennifer is engulfed.

Eddie cringes. Pain from the vampires blow shoots down the entire length of his back. He gets to his knees and receives a boot to his stomach for his efforts.

"Lewis wasn't a punter," is all he can choke out.

Then he remembers it: if he can just get to the hall-way that led to the balcony... He thought it odd when he passed it the first time, but now realizes that maybe it was part of God's plan.

The level of black smoke in the room increases and he uses the distraction to crawl to the hallway exit. He gets to his feet and stands against the far wall coughing loudly enough that the other vampire will know his exact location. Then, just as he had prayed would happen, vampire Ray Lewis begins to walk through the wall opposite him. Lewis never makes it to Eddie though, because staring at Eddie across the hall was the mounted head of an African Elephant complete with ivory tusks that the other vampire had just inadvertently impaled himself on.

Eddie scrambles back into the ballroom and sprouts his wings in an attempt to get above the smoke and get a better view of his enemies. As soon as he rises above it, though, the smoke begins to dissipate.

Jennifer—using her incredible speed, runs back and forth fast enough to create enough wind to push the smoke from the room.

"That's all you got, bitch?" Jennifer laughs and strikes vampire Ursula in the back, reaching through and clutching her heart in her hand. Before Ursula can gargle an answer, Jennifer swings her hand violently across her body and removes the vampire's head.

Then a shriek pierces the room and Jennifer and Eddie turn to find Lisa squeezing Courtney's heart tightly in her fist. It's an empty threat meant to make Jennifer pause before killing anyone else.

"You wouldn't." Jennifer tries to sound calm as she stares into Lisa's icy eyes.

"I can only be pushed so far without retaliation. You have killed too many of my progeny, Jennifer."

Eddie begins to fly closer.

"Ah-ah-ah, Slayer. An inch closer and the head comes off."

Eddie freezes, and then another scream catches everyone's attention. Apparently, Evil has had enough with the toying around as she now has Taryn by the neck—with both Taryn's feet off the ground.

Molly begins to shake uncontrollably. Eddie begins to move toward her, but simultaneous screams of "No!" from behind him stop him in his tracks. When he turns around, Lisa is still holding Courtney's heart, agony on her face. Perry's Bride of Dracula is holding Courtney's severed head in one hand and Perry's hand in the other.

Jennifer is there, too, with her hand through Bride of Dracula's chest.

Perry is only partially present. His arm and the hand holding his bride are all that are visible.

To Eddie it seems that this image is lasting an eternity. As if time has frozen in this moment of atrocity.

"Eddie?"

The voice catches Eddie by surprise.

"What's wrong with everyone?" It's Molly, and she's moving toward him while everything else remains frozen in time. Eddie flies down to meet her.

She stares at his wings. "So, you're an angel or something?"

"Something," Eddie replies under his breath. "Did you...?"

"Yeah; I think so." She beams.

"Well, whatever you did, keep it that way as long as you can." He flies closer to Jennifer and the horrifying scene around her. He grabs Perry's arm in hopes of pulling him back, but the arm comes free of whatever was tethering it to Perry's new location. In frustration, Eddie swings it at Dracula's bride's head, and removes it in the process. He turns when he hears Molly grunt as she breaks Evil's hands off one by one and gently lies Taryn on the ground.

"Eddie!" Molly stares at him wide-eyed as she begins to shake uncontrollably again.

Suddenly the world is alive again. Evil screams in agony as she bleeds out from the places that her hands used to be.

Molly stands between her and the apples; Evil cannot seem to regenerate without them. Adam lets out a throaty groan before fleeing to the closest exit.

Lisa is overcome by emotion as she takes in the carnage around her. She falls to the ground, bawling. Jennifer too, is overcome with sadness. She drops the heart that she was holding and falls to her knees, attempting to cradle the dust that was once Courtney's body.

"Eddie! Mom! She's not breathing."

The Editor

Molly's voice is but a distant echo as Eddie tries to make sense of all that's going on around him.

Chapter 74

Lincoln and Abby sit at the table talking about possible solutions to the ghost pirate dilemma while Jack drinks the rum, *sans glass*. Beth seems to have abandoned hope—or at the very least lost interest—as she's moved to the couch where Noel is asleep on her lap. She flips through the stations, trying to find something to watch on the television

"Oh! Oh! That's it," Jack slurs as he points to the television and begins to laugh.

"What?" Lincoln and Abby shout in unison.

"On the box there. Those ladies with the humorous clothing. They *bust ghosts.*" Jack again bursts into drunken laughter that doesn't end until he begins to hiccup.

Beth puts her head on the table in exhaustion.

"Jack, we need you to take this seriously. If we don't find a way to get rid of them, they'll hurt more innocent people. I know that you don't want that. I wrote...they took you against your will. You know the unspeakable things that they're capable of. Please? Anything you can think of would help."

Jack glares at Lincoln. "Get rid of them, mate? What you're asking me to do is get rid of meself, as well."

Before Lincoln can even respond, Jack glances in Noel's direction and smiles. "But I know a way, and fortunately for you, you wrote me to be pretty valiant once I get some rum in me. So, listen close, ya' hear?"

Chapter 75

Eddie emerges from the mental fog and catches sight of Molly with her bloody wrist pressed against Taryn's mouth. "Molly, wait!" He starts in her direction, but realizes that either way, it's too late. Instead, he flies over to Jennifer and Lisa who are both still weeping uncontrollably.

"G-g-go ahead. I have no desire to live in this world," Lisa eventually manages. Eddie is happy to oblige and reaches into her chest until he can feel his hand close around her beating heart.

"Stop," Jennifer whispers. Both Eddie and Lisa's heads snap in her direction. "He broke your bond, right?" Jennifer stares at Lisa, already knowing the answer.

Lisa nods in confirmation.

"Why would he do that? He needs allies." Eddie looks from one vampire to the other.

"Too much history," Lisa whispers. "He wanted to kill Courtney straight away, but I convinced him to wait... told him that if we killed Jenny, she would come back to us—to me. Now his mate is dead and he blames me." Lisa's eyes shift to what Eddie holds in his right hand and she pauses before raising an eyebrow. "Is that Perry's arm?"

Eddie looks back at Molly, who still has her wrist pressed against Taryn's mouth and is still crying for Jennifer to help her.

"Um, yeah." He nods to Jennifer, urging her to help Molly. Before he can even finish the nod though, Jennifer is there at her progeny's side.

"Are you trying to drown her?" She pulls Molly's wrist away from Taryn's mouth. She feels Taryn's neck for a pulse and shoots Eddie a look. "Burn the arm and meet us back at the room."

Molly's voice shakes. "Mom, what about Taryn. Will she...?"

"We wait and see." She lifts Taryn's lifeless body from the floor.

She's almost out the door before Eddie can get the words out. "What about Lisa?"

"Whatever you think," she answers as if he asked her which hat to buy.

Eddie turns to Lisa, who hangs her head. His natural slayer instincts tell him to end the creature here and now, but he's never killed anyone who was not an imminent threat to himself— or to the innocent. He's not sure that Lisa poses any such threat anymore.

"Whatever I think," he whispers.

Chapter 76

Lincoln nudges Abby who almost jumps out of her seat. "What!? What'd I miss?"

"Jack has a plan." Lincoln grins and gently nods towards Jack.

"Sure enough, I think I've figured a way," Jack starts before swallowing the last of the rum. "Ya see, those fellas are only after one thing. The desire to find that thing is what fuels their—*our*—spirits."

"Treasure." Abby sticks out her tongue and rolls her eyes.

Jack smiles and tries to take another swig from the empty bottle. He frowns when he realizes that there's nothing left and closes his eyes trying to regain his train of thought.

Lincoln shakes his head. "No... fame. They wanted to be the most famous pirate crew of all time."

"Aye." Jack nods. "It's why they brought me along. They needed me to document their travels."

"So, you think if they—*you*— become famous, you'll disappear?"

"Aye. I've felt it. Every time we raid, more people believe in us, and I feel my tie to the physical world decrease. But once we go back out to sea and people begin to question or doubt exactly what happened, the tie gets stronger again and the captain finds a new spot to raid."

Abby scowls at Jack. "So, we need to let you commit crimes so heinous that you become the most infamous pirate crew ever?"

Jack shrugs.

"I really should have put more effort into this story," Lincoln runs his hands through his hair. "But I think I have an idea. Jack, can you take me to your captain?"

"Aye." Jack nods. "I'll be needin' some more rum for the trip, though."

"Us," Abby chimes in. "Take *us* to your captain."

Chapter 77

"I'm sorry," Eddie's voice cracks as he readies himself.

Lisa smiles back at him. "Don't be. I deserve worse."

Eddie pulls back his fist before driving into her chest for the second time that night.

"I wouldn't do that. She may be of great use to your cause." The voice comes from the far side of the room. The priest from earlier steps over the piles of ash that were once Courtney and Perry's latest mate. Eddie and Lisa both turn to face the priest, each as confused as the other.

"Father." Eddie nods towards the man. "No offense, but how could you know...?"

The priest points to the ceiling. "Direct line." He laughs. "I think your friend in the Caribbean explained some of this to you, right?"

Eddie thinks back to what Lincoln showed him about Jophiel, and slowly removes his hand from Lisa's chest, leaving her heart in place.

"So, I'm a little lost here." Lisa's eyes shift from Eddie to the priest.

The priest smiles and lifts his hands to the sides of her face. "May I?"

Lisa shrugs. "What's the worst that can happen?"

The priest grabs her gently by the head. Lisa's vision goes blurry before she is engulfed by a blinding white light.

Eddie stares at Lisa as she shivers uncontrollably in the priest's grasp. He wonders if this is what an exorcism looks like but before he knows it, the priest stops, turns and walks back across the room and up the stairs toward where he'd first met Eddie and Jennifer.

Lisa blinks repeatedly as if trying to get something out of her eye before turning to Eddie. "He's right, you can't kill me. You need me." She brushes past Eddie headed toward the door.

"Says the evil vampire who I was about to kill," Eddie cackles mockingly.

Lisa stops when he says *evil,* as if the word literally pierces her. "I'm sorry. For everything," she whispers before continuing to the exit that Jennifer and Molly had taken earlier.

He can't explain how, but Eddie knows that she means it. "Wait! Okay, but where are you going?" he calls out from behind her.

The Editor

"Your hotel," she says, not breaking stride.

"But how?"

"He showed me many things. Now, come on. We don't have much time."

Eddie can't help it. His curiosity gets the better of him and he hesitantly follows his enemy out of the church.

Chapter 78

The next day is a fairly normal day of vacation for everyone, except Jack, of course. Lincoln takes Noel to the water park where they spend most of the day. Abby and Beth cozy up next to each other under the most majestic palm tree that either has ever seen. Jack stays back in the condo, enjoying every second that he is not on the ship or with the other ghosts. An odd sensation washes over him repeatedly throughout the day though; almost like waves of emptiness crashing into his chest.

Just before sunset, Lincoln and Noel meet Beth and Abby for dinner at a small Irish-style pub on the resort.

"Figured we'd eat here since we didn't get to go to Dublin." Lincoln pulls out a chair for each of the women.

"Somehow, I think we probably got the better end of that deal." Beth grins and kisses Lincoln on the cheek.

Lincoln almost asks out loud if that means she has forgiven him, but thinks better of it and instead just clears his throat and smiles back.

The dinner conversation is pretty much dominated by Noel, who excitedly recaps just about every minute of their water park adventure. Everyone else laughs at her story, but the nervous energy is evident. After dinner, they walk back to the condo, with Noel still chattering about the slides at the water park.

Jack is waiting for Lincoln and Abby at the door, so they say their goodbyes quickly.

"Beth, if anything seems wrong," Lincoln looks away.

"I'll protect her with my life, Lincoln. Just try not to let things go wrong." She winks before giving him an awkward hug.

Lincoln, Abby and Jack make their way carefully to the beach, trying to keep Jack as hidden as possible, where they push a Hobie Cat into the surf. Abby calls for a gentle wind to guide them out into the water.

"Same place that ya found us last night." Jack points northeast. "Ship should be good as new."

The water is calm as they make their way further and further from the island. It's a beautiful, starry night and the only wind is that being manufactured by Abby.

"We're close. I can feel it in me chest," Jack utters just before *The Bearded Ghost* suddenly appears directly in front of them. Abby quickly changes the direction of the wind and sail to avoid running into the bow of the ship.

"Garrgh! It's the poet!" someone on the ship shouts.

"Throw down the ropes!" Jack calls back.

A rope with knots tied in it every few feet is lowered and Jack grabs hold, using it to climb the side of the ship. "Follow me." He keeps climbing without looking back.

Abby motions for Lincoln to go first, probably so that she can help him if needed, and he doesn't argue. Jack scales the side of the ship with little difficulty, but the same cannot be said for Lincoln. Eventually, though, Lincoln makes it to the top. Abby gives him a shove with her free hand and he spills onto the ship's deck. Abby hops over nimbly and hoists Lincoln to his feet. Forty sets of angry glowing eyes stare back at them.

A woman steps forward and addresses Jack. "Who are the scallywags and where uv' ye been, Black Jack?"

"Did that bitch just call me a scallywag?" Abby's voice is a little too loud, and much too angry for Lincoln's liking.

The Editor

Jack quickly answers. "'Ello, Captain Merrick." Jack removes his hat and bows before addressing the woman. "These are me mates, Abby and Lincoln. They rescued me last night and have an interesting proposition for the crew of *The Bearded Ghost.*"

Captain Merrick glares at Abby, before offering a smile at Lincoln and extending him her hand to kiss. "You, my good sir, can call me Pearl."

Lincoln throws Abby a sideways glance and kisses the captain's glowing hand.

"Follow me," Captain Merrick takes Lincoln's hand in her own as the crew parts, allowing her to walk toward the ship's cabin.

Chapter 79

Eddie is barely able to keep up with Lisa on the way back to the hotel. He's happy to stay a few steps behind her, though, so that he can make sure she really *does* know where they're staying. She walks into the hotel without hesitation and directly up to the exact room that he and Jennifer have rented under a false name.

She smirks. "Shall I knock, or do you have a key?"

"Whose room is this?" Eddie shrugs his shoulders, pretending to be confused.

Lisa rolls her eyes and knocks on the door confidently. Molly answers, and the shock of seeing Lisa must activate her power, because soon, Eddie and Molly are the only two moving.

"Hey, Molly, loving this power but I kind of need to talk to Jenny, now. So, can you cut it out?"

"I... I dunno what the feck I'm doin', Eddie. And why don't you freeze by tha' way?"

Eddie walks over and pours himself a double shot of bourbon. "I'm special, I guess." He winks before swallowing a mouthful. Eddie snaps his fingers and the room comes back to life. "No shit. Didn't really think that was gonna work." He puts an arm around Jennifer.

Jennifer looks momentarily confused before realizing what happened. Soon her eyes fall on Lisa, who made her way to the corner of the room farthest away from Jennifer.

"I see you didn't kill her. What'd she do... beg? Make you *promises*?" Jennifer asks accusingly.

Eddie throws up his hands in surrender. "The priest—" he starts before Lisa cuts him off.

"We don't have time for this petty jealousy. The priest showed me a vision. We need to get to the author and reverse the stupidity that he's set in motion," Lisa says, as if there was no other option.

"Um, no," Jennifer huffs. "Lincoln and Abby can handle themselves. We're finishing what we started with Perry."

"And Adam," Molly quickly adds.

Lisa shakes her head in disapproval. "Perry has Adam and they went east to recruit and/or make new friends. Trust me, I want them dead as much as you do, but the matter in the Caribbean is much more important right now."

"Who made this eejit Queen?" Molly bares her fangs at Lisa.

"She knew our hotel and exact room number without hesitation. She knows where Lincoln is. The priest had to have shown her *something*," Eddie tries to explain calmly.

Suddenly a gurgling sound from the bed grabs everyone's attention.

"Taryn!!" Molly shouts excitedly. "She's alive!"

"And she's going to be hungry," Jennifer says, moving protectively in front of Eddie.

Eddie raises an eyebrow. "What? I can handle myself."

"She still needs to eat," Jennifer says dismissively. "Lisa, can I trust you to bring us a few, um, snacks? *No killing.*"

Lisa sighs and starts toward the door. "I've never been one to show restraint, but I guess I'm willing to learn."

"Then I *guess* I'll let you live," Jennifer mutters as Lisa closes the door behind her.

Jennifer shakes her head, trying to make sense of everything that has happened in the last thirty-six hours. While they wait for Lisa to return, Jennifer and Molly tend to Taryn, who is unusually quiet. Eddie pours himself another glass of bourbon and lets Jennifer deal with baby vampires.

The Editor

Soon the sound of flirtatious giggling fills the hall-way and there's a soft knock on the door. Lisa opens it without waiting for anyone to answer.

"See, boys? Didn't I tell you they were *drop-dead gorgeous?*"

Chapter 80

Captain Merrick stops short of the cabin door. "The lady waits here. I'm sure me crew can keep 'er entertained."

Abby nods confidently at Lincoln, who follows Merrick and Jack into the captain's quarters.

"Black Jack, this better be worth me time." She pulls a wooden chair up to a small round table. She leans back in the chair and props her feet on the table, boots and all.

Captain Merrick is a bigger woman—not obese—but definitely full-figured. You can tell that she is confident in her body by the way she carries herself; she walks tall and speaks confidently. Lincoln can't help but feel somewhat proud of her.

She removes her coat, revealing a more than ample chest, which puts a few other thoughts in Lincoln's mind. Her red hair gives her a glow that separates her from the rest of her crew; that and the fact that she's the only one who seems to have a full set of teeth.

"Well, which of ye scallywags is gonna do the talkin'?"

"Aye, Captain. This is gonna come as a bit of a shock to ya, but you know how on the past few raids things have seemed a wee bit... *different?*" Jack stops, trying to find the right way to explain things.

Lincoln watches Captain Merrick's eyes shift downward and they both wait for Jack to continue.

"Well, we be characters from a story. The world seems a wee bit curious because our story takes place a long time ago. If that be makin' any sense?"

Captain Merrick eyes Jack and then Lincoln, before she bursts into raucous laughter.

"It's true." Lincoln hesitates, but then he pulls out his phone. Thankfully, he had thought to snap a few screenshots of his book before they left the island since he has no service this far out at sea.

"Oh, because you say so?" Captain Merrick laughs.

"Because I'm the author." He tosses his phone to her. She quickly dodges the phone and draws her sword. Lincoln throws his hand up in surrender.

"No, no, no. Just look at it. It's like a... picture machine."

The captain slowly re-sheaths her sword, steps over to the phone, and carefully picks it up. "Show me." She holds the phone out to Lincoln.

Lincoln approaches her carefully and turns on the screen, which thankfully still works. He'd never been so happy that he bought the LifeProof case for his phone. He scrolls through a few screenshots of the story.

"Won't do me much good—seein' as I can't read," she huffs.

"Just wait." Lincoln continues to scroll through the screenshots until he finds a drawing that is clearly Captain Pearl Merrick. She gasps at the image of herself. Lincoln scrolls some more until another picture appears— Black Jack being taken captive.

"Why does the poet get a portrait?" she scoffs.

Lincoln smirks at Jack.

"So, me and me crew, we're famous?" Her eyes glow even brighter.

Lincoln grimaces. "Well, not exactly. Yet. But with the help of this," he holds up his phone, "... if you trust me, you'll be the *most* famous pirate crew in all of history. All we have to do is aim this device at you and we can record whatever we want. Then with the touch of a button, I can send it to the world. Then, bam! You're instantaneously famous!"

The captain closes her eyes and leans back in her chair. "Hmmm. Let me think about it. We'll hold off on tonight's raid. Black Jack, take the wench and feed her.

This one will dine with me. Some more *conversation* may help me make me decision."

Jack casts Lincoln a pitying glance before he gets up and heads to the door.

"Captain— I mean, Pearl." Lincoln smiles shyly. "May I speak to my friend before she eats?"

"Make it quick. I've got plans for you." The captain slowly runs her tongue around her puffy lips.

Lincoln feels a sense of nervous excitement as he makes his way to the cabin door. He pokes his head outside where Abby is waiting alongside Jack, and two of the scarier looking pirates.

"Just eat what they give you," he whispers in her ear. "We wouldn't want them getting the wrong idea."

"What are you doing?" She raises her eyebrows. "Aren't you coming?"

"Closing the deal," he mutters before ducking back into the captain's quarters.

Abby could swear that she saw a smile on his face just before the door shuts.

Chapter 81

"I found these gentleman downstairs and they assured me that they know how to show a woman a good time." Lisa winks.

Eddie looks at Jennifer with wide eyes. She gives him a nod signifying she has the situation under control.

"I'm gonna grab a refill downstairs." Eddie holds up his nearly empty bourbon bottle.

One of the men, a silver-haired man of about fifty with an American southern accent, holds out a hundred dollar bill. "You do that, friend. We'll take good care of the girls." He licks his lips as he says it. "Be a champ and grab us a bottle of their best champagne while you're down there."

Eddie pockets the money and rolls his eyes. "Okay, sport."

When Eddie returns to the room with his bottle of bourbon— and what was left of the man's money in his pocket— the three other men are waiting in the hall, staring into nothingness.

As Eddie approaches them, the one closest asks, "Are you Eddie?" His voice is oddly monotone, with a southern accent like the silver-haired man, who is apparently still inside.

"Yep."

"She said we had to ask you where to go before we can leave."

Eddie thinks for a moment and laughs. "Church sounds about right. Your pick on which one though."

The three men leave without hesitation and walk down the hall like a small herd of zombies.

Eddie opens the door to find Lisa and Jennifer sitting across from each other at the table, deep in conversation. The sound of running water comes from the bathroom, and Molly is nowhere to be found, so he assumes that she's in there. Then his eyes fall to the bed and to Taryn, who is apparently draining every last drop of blood from the silver-haired fox.

Eddie's facial muscles tighten. "Jenny! What the...?"

"He was an ass. He's married *and* he slapped Taryn across the face and called her a whore as soon as you left."

"Okay, so you teach him a lesson. You don't KILL him!"

"He barely has any caffeine in his system. She needed all of the blood." Jennifer flips her hand dismissively, sounding disinterested.

"For the love of... We can't just pick and choose who deserves to live and die."

Lisa, seemingly annoyed that Eddie interrupted her conversation with Jennifer, glances up. "And there's also this." She tosses something in Eddie's direction. "It's the dick's phone."

Eddie stares at the display and immediately drops the phone in disgust. "She can't be more than... Fuck it, let's pack up. Leave the phone next to him on the bed. I'm sure it'll make finding his killer less of a priority."

"Lisa got us tickets to Turks and Caicos first thing in the morning, but we can't get there until tomorrow night. She said Lincoln and Abby will need to buy some time in order for us to make it over there to help them." Jennifer places a comforting hand on Eddie's back.

Eddie closes his eyes, enjoying the feel of Jennifer's touch. "Molly and Taryn... Will they be okay leaving here? We could really use Molly's power, especially if you can teach her how to use it right."

Jennifer nods. "Taryn may be hard to control on the plane, but Molly has adapted rather quickly and she gave Taryn her blood, so hopefully she will as well. In any case, Lisa and I can handle it."

The Editor

"And what? You two are like best friends again?"

Jennifer sighs. "Eddie, she had no choice until the bond with Perry was broken. Had he not broken my bond earlier, I would've been in the same position. I'm willing to give her a chance and I want you to do the same."

Eddie shakes his head. "Whatever. I don't have a problem with giving her a chance, I just don't see the need to be all buddy-buddy with her."

Jennifer kisses Eddie passionately on the lips setting off a series of internal explosions. It's the only thing he craves more than bourbon.

"Just try, sweetie. For me. For Courtney," she chokes out as a tear rolls slowly down her cheek.

Chapter 82

Lincoln lies awake but with his eyes closed, strangely satisfied after a night with Captain Merrick. Suddenly a groaning sound, followed by a loud bang startles him fully awake. It's not until he opens his eyes that he realizes how uncomfortable he is. His hands are chained to the wall above his head and he was sleeping propped up against a wooden crate— in a dark cell of some sort.

As his vision becomes clearer, the same scary looking ghost pirates escort Abby into the cell with him. Abby sashays in with her head held high, while the pirates limp in, being sure to stay at a safe distance behind her. The pirates chain Abby up across the cell from Lincoln and promptly leave.

"W-where am I?" Lincoln asks, rubbing his eyes against his shoulders as he attempts to clear his mind. "Man, my head hasn't throbbed like this since... well, actually this is pretty common for me, but it still sucks."

Abby chuckles. "Well Casanova, you're in what I believe they call *the brig*."

The Editor

"Well, why are you here? I mean, you could've escaped. Are you okay? Did they hurt—"

"I had to find your horny ass. I mean, I wasn't just going to leave you here. And I'm fine. They only brought me here because I wanted them to."

Lincoln groans and rubs his forehead. "Much appreciated. What happened?"

Abby laughs. "I guess you're not as much of a Lothario as you thought. I overheard the guards saying something about the Captain telling them to head to shore, but then a one-armed man just appeared out of nowhere and talked to the Captain, and she had you thrown in the brig. That's when I picked a fight with those two so I could come rescue you. So, was it worth it?"

Lincoln blushes and shrugs. "Umm, a gentleman never tells?"

"Yeah, whatever. You ready for me to bust us out of here?"

Lincoln closes his eyes again, trying to focus. "Not yet. We need more information. Let me try to contact Eddie."

Eddie. Eddie?

Lincoln waits, but hears no reply. "It's my head. It's so foggy. Let me try again."

Eddie? Eddie!

Ouch. Damnit, Lincoln! Why are you yelling? And what is wrong with your thinking voice?

Long story...

Oh shit! With a ghost pirate? You dog. She's not too shabby either, for a ghost... and a pirate.

Funny, Eddie. So, as you can likely sense, we're in some trouble here. I had the ghost pirates right where I wanted them—

Yeah, you did. Hahahaha!

Anyways... Apparently some one-armed guy shows up out of nowhere and changes the Captain's mind. I never created any one-armed characters.

Yeah, but I did. Ripped Perry's arm off yesterday. Long story. Cliff notes are: Lisa is with us now. Have two newbie vamps— one has a kick ass power that can help with Perry's annoying ability to disappear and reappear whenever and wherever he'd like, hence the one arm thing. Any chance you can hold them off for six hours or so, until we can get to the resort?"

What time of day is it?

Around one p.m. your time, I think.

Yeah, just get here as soon as you can. If we escape now, they'll be at full strength to attack again tonight.

Okay, have me some of the good stuff waiting. They only have scotch on the plane.

The Editor

"Okay Abby, let's get the heck outta here. And you need to sink the ship when we do."

"Sounds like fun." She snaps her restraints like they were made of paper.

Chapter 83

Abby frees Lincoln from his restraints and helps him to his feet. She scans the room and notices a few barrels sitting against a wall in the far corner. "Help me push those barrels over here. We'll bind them together with the chains and that rope. Then climb on top and hang on."

It takes a few minutes, but they build a makeshift raft from the barrels. Lincoln leans against one of the barrels, exhausted, and watches Abby put the finishing touches on the raft. He's sweating through his clothes and she is still a picture of perfection. Not even a hair out of place. Lincoln climbs atop and closes his eyes.

"I'm ready." His voice shakes.

Abby leaps atop the raft with panther-like agility and raises her hands above her head. A swirling wind begins to blow through the brig and the ships' wooden hull begins to creak. She slams her hands down to her sides and a burst of thunder shakes the entire ship. Lincoln can smell burning wood. Nails begin to pop all over the ship. Water starts to trickle into the brig.

"Hold on," Abby yells over the sounds of thunder, water, and screaming ghost pirates. She makes a parting motion with her hands and a ferocious wind tears apart the starboard side of the ship. Water rushes in, and suddenly the raft is on its way out to sea. Waves crash over the raft, but Abby helps keep Lincoln on board. As he wipes the salt water out of his eyes, he looks out at the terrified glowing faces of drowning ghost pirates and, for just a moment, a wave a guilt washes over him.

"Jack," he gasps as another wave smashes against his side, nearly knocking him from Abby's grasp.

"He'll be back tomorrow." Without a second thought, Abby places her hands into the water and the waves around the raft seem to calm and then act as a motor, guiding the raft back to what Lincoln hopes is the coastline. "Just try to relax. We'll be back to the condo soon."

'

Chapter 84

"So, I take it that it went well?" Beth kisses Abby on the cheek.

"Papa!" Noel shrieks as she runs to Lincoln and hugs him tightly. "Can we go to the water park again today?"

"Sure, sweetie. Go get your suit on," Lincoln says, allowing the adults a few minutes to discuss what happened.

"Didn't go exactly as planned." Lincoln's face tightens as he addresses Beth's question.

Beth bites her lip. "So, what do we do now?" She shifts her gaze frantically from Abby to Lincoln, waiting for a solution.

Lincoln rubs the back of his neck. "Get a bottle of bourbon ready. Eddie should be here around dinner time and he's bringing help."

"I'm starving. Destroying the ship again took a lot out of me." Abby plops down on the tweed couch.

"I just had a cup of coffee." Beth sits down next to her and offers her wrist.

The Editor

Abby glances at Lincoln who quickly turns away.

Beth glares at Lincoln. "What? We're imprinted. She won't hurt me and you *will* need her help tonight. Take Noel to grab some pizza and enjoy the water park. By the time you get back, Abby will be back at full strength."

Lincoln can't argue with her logic, so he heads to grab his swimsuit and some sunscreen.

The day goes by much too quickly for Lincoln's liking. After grabbing pizza and spending the day between the water park and the beach, Lincoln and Noel finally head back to the condo. They need to shower before Eddie and the others arrive, so that they can all grab dinner and formally brief each other on everything that's happened.

"Papa?" Noel looks up at Lincoln while shielding her eyes from the setting sun. "Are we going to be okay?"

Lincoln tries to hide his nervousness. "What do you mean, sweetie? Of course we're going to be okay."

Noel smiles and grabs Lincoln's hand. "You, Aunt Beth, and Miss Abby all seem so worried here. And what happened to Mr. Jack?"

Lincoln wipes some sweat from his forehead. "It's just some grown-up stuff, sweetie. Eddie is coming to help me sort it all out. You just need to focus on having fun and conquering that big waterslide tomorrow," Lincoln says, trying to convince himself that he's not lying to his daughter.

"Eddie's coming? Awesome!" Noel jumps up and down a few times before she skips through the door and heads straight for the shower.

Beth and Abby are both already ready and they both look incredible. Beth is wearing a bright-colored sundress and has her hair crimped, which was always how Lincoln liked it best. Abby has on a tight black cocktail dress and has her hair up in a high bun.

Lincoln has to remind himself to close his jaw. "Wow, you ladies look fantastic." Both women look at each other and grin.

"Jennifer called; said they're on the shuttle. They should be here any minute." Abby walks over to the kitchenette and fixes Beth a martini.

She's been playing everything cool, but Lincoln can hear a hint of nerves in her voice now. He hands her the jar of olives. "Yeah, Eddie told me. I asked him to have someone give you all a heads up in case you were..." His voice trails off at the end.

Beth laughs. "How considerate of you. Well, you better hurry up and shower. And put something nice on today— no flip-flops. We have reservations at the Italian restaurant in a half hour."

The Editor

"I don't have anything *that* nice," Lincoln mutters as he heads into his bedroom.

Chapter 85

When Lincoln finally emerges from the bedroom dressed in a black and white button-down shirt and black slacks, he finds everyone gathered in the condo's kitchen having a lively discussion.

Noel, who is wearing a beautiful sundress of her own, is telling a story from earlier that day at the water park. "... and then the raft tipped over and papa got stuck, and he came up and was splashing all around and accidentally knocked over this other pretty lady's raft, and she was like, *"Eek! I can't believe you got my hair wet,"* and Papa was like, *"we ARE at a water park... ha ha ha."* Then they both started laughing. I think she liked him."

"Clumsy charm? Yep, that's your dad." Beth scoops her niece up in her arms.

Lincoln smiles as he overhears the conversation.

"Well, if it ain't the king of smooth himself." Eddie raises his glass of bourbon in Lincoln's direction. "Let's go eat."

Abby, undoubtedly using mind control, reserved the entire Italian restaurant for them from 7:30 until 9:30. They all sit around a large rectangular table where a family-style meal is served to them by a most gracious staff.

"So, everyone, this is Molly. She can freeze time." Eddie pauses dramatically, allowing the statement to take hold. "Molly, this is everyone. Abby over there can summon the weather. Lincoln writes bad books, Beth is the glue that keeps all of them together and Abby's imprint, and little Noel there can melt hearts... figuratively, of course."

Jennifer smacks Eddie on the arm. "You didn't tell me they imprinted! Congratulations, you two!" She beams across the table.

"Sorry, love. Busy saving the world and making friends with enemies and stuff. Speaking of. You all know Lisa." He motions to the far end of the table, drawing a shy wave from Lisa. "And this is Taryn, Molly's BFF, new vampire. She was quite aggressive as a human, but has yet to speak as a vampire." Taryn smiles as Molly puts her arm around her.

"Where's Courtney?" Beth asks as if just noticing she's not there.

"Excuse me." Jennifer gets up from the table and quickly makes her way to the bathroom. Abby and

Beth's expressions go from confusion, to realization, and finally to sadness.

"She's, um—" Eddie starts.

"She's in Heaven," Lisa says calmly before going back to buttering her bread.

Eddie gawks at her, half thankful, half like she's crazy.

Lisa continues buttering the bread. "The priest showed me as much."

"Damnit Eddie, a heads-up would've been nice." Lincoln shakes his head. "I mean, you never even *thought* it. Go check on her, dummy!"

Everyone is quiet and picks at their salads until Eddie and Jennifer return. Jennifer's demeanor seems to be much improved. She places a hand on Lisa's shoulder and mouths "thank you."

"So, the weather here beats Dublin." Jennifer attempts to lighten the mood. This leads to a detailed conversation about their time in Dublin and some of what has happened on the island. Everyone particularly gets a kick out of Abby's exaggerated, yet G-rated story of Lincoln's love affair with Captain Pearl Merrick during the main course of dinner.

"Okay, okay, okay." Lincoln tries to quell everyone's laughter. He pulls out his cell phone to check the time. "The pirates should make landfall less than a mile from here in about ninety minutes according to Jophiel's vision. We need a plan."

Chapter 86

"Okay, so theoretically I can kill the ghost pirates, right? I'm just not sure how," Eddie starts as the waiter brings him another glass of bourbon. "What about the vamps? Can they do any damage?"

Abby nods as she swallows a mouthful of gnocchi. "We can kill them temporarily, but they would be back the next evening when the ship regenerates. But if nothing else, we can help hold them off until you can finish them."

"Plus, we can kill Perry," Jennifer adds stoically.

"Okay, then. I think we should attempt to draw them onto land so that we don't risk losing any of them at sea." Lincoln stands and pushes his chair back from the table. "I know the place, I saw it in the vision. It didn't make sense at the time, but it's perfect."

Beth raises her eyebrows. "You're leaving now?"

"Heading back to the condo to change and get supplies."

"Let's go." Eddie gets up to follow Lincoln out. Everyone else begins to push away from the table as well.

The Editor

Noel walks over to the new vampires and smiles. "Nice to meet you." She holds a hand out to Molly, who takes it and returns her smile.

"You *are* a wee heart melter, aren't ya?"

Noel then extends a hand to Taryn. "Hello." When she takes Taryn's hand, she gasps and steps back, but doesn't let go. The look of terror soon melts into a smile and tears begin to well up in her eyes. She surges forward and wraps both arms around the vampire. "Mommy!"

Chapter 87

Lincoln stops and whirls around to find Sara holding Noel's tiny face in her hands. Molly is standing next to her, eyes and mouth wide open, so Lincoln knows that she sees the change as well.

Sara kisses Noel on the forehead. "Hello, baby cakes."

"It *is* you!" Noel shrieks. "Mommy, mommy! I have a daddy!"

A tear falls down Sara's left cheek and onto the ground as everyone else stands around in amazement.

"Yes sweetie, it is me, in a way. And yes, you *do* have a daddy." She glances at Lincoln, then at Beth, expecting to see anger in their eyes. Instead, she's met by stares of wonder and longing, respectively.

"I don't have a lot of time, but I want you to know that I'm doing great. I miss you terribly, but I'm always watching you and now, thanks to the power that God gave Miss Taryn, we can visit each other any time that you would like to— as long as it's okay with Miss

Taryn." She bends down again to kiss Noel on the forehead and squeezes her in a mother's embrace.

"Beth, I'm sorry. There's no explanation that I can give you that makes what Lincoln and I did okay, but God certainly doesn't waste anything. Look at the good that has come out of our mistake." She looks first at Noel, then at Abby. "Abby, take care of my sister." She winks at her sister's soulmate.

"And Lincoln." Sara clears her throat. "Perhaps I most owe an apology to you. I took advantage of a bad time for you and for that, I'm sorry. But I'm even more sorry that I let my fear keep you from your amazing daughter for so long. I hope that you can someday forgive me." Her tone is sincere and Lincoln can't find any words, so instead he just nods and smiles weakly.

Sara again squeezes Noel tightly. "Okay, baby doll. Miss Taryn is getting really tired now so I have to go for a while." She lifts Noel so that their eyes meet and hugs her tightly against her chest. "I love you so much."

"Mommy, no! Don't go!" But by the time the tears in Noel's eyes dry, Taryn is back and looking worse for the wear.

Eddie pulls Noel out of Taryn's embrace. "Lisa, Molly, get her back to the condo and find her some-one— *something*— to eat."

Lincoln, stilled stunned by what had just taken place, begins to stammer. "O-okay, let's move."

Chapter 88

No one says a word about Taryn's apparent power as they pile back into the condo, but it's most obviously on everyone's mind.

Eddie pours himself a drink and takes a sip, letting it linger in his mouth a while before finally swallowing and savoring the burning trail that the bourbon leaves down the back of his throat.

"Okay, everyone. We have a battle to win, a world to save, so you all need to focus. Lincoln, what's the plan?"

Lincoln's head snaps up, as if Eddie had just startled him awake from a dream that he didn't want to stop having. "Oh, umm... well, Eddie, I think this plan has gotta be on you. I mean, you're the only one who can actually stop the ghost pirates. What do you think?"

Eddie relishes the opportunity to be a warrior, but is not as comfortable making decisions that could put others at risk. "Feck." He shakes his head and draws confused looks from Lincoln, Beth, and Abby. He laughs.

"Just something I picked up over in Ireland. And don't you go repeating that either." He glances over at Noel.

"Okay, so we know that I can defeat the ghost pirates, we just don't know how. Abby has been effective in holding them off so far, so taking her with me is probably a good idea. Molly is our only hope of catching Perry so she's in."

"I'm going if she goes." Taryn perks up some after feeding on whoever— or whatever— Lisa and Molly had found for her. Before anyone can protest, she holds up a hand. "Wasn't up for discussion."

"I didn't know who she was at the time, but she was in the vision," Lincoln says softly.

"Yes. Taryn is important," Lisa adds.

"Well, how does she help?" Eddie asks.

Lincoln and Lisa look at each other before Lincoln answers. "The visions don't work like that."

"Useful," Eddie mocks. "Anyways, I'll need a vamp to stay back and help Lincoln protect Beth and Noel and the rest of the island, I guess. So, Jenny, you'll need to stay here." Eddie knows that he's selfishly keeping Jennifer out of harm's way and when she tries to protest he quickly shuts it down. "You're strong and fast enough to carry both Beth and Noel away from any danger while Lincoln fights off whatever he can."

Lincoln clears his throat. "Actually—"

The Editor

"Damnit Lincoln, you said I was making the plans, so Jenny stays!"

Lincoln stands. "I don't disagree with Jennifer staying, but I have to go. It's me that has to kill Perry." He stares at the floor, not sure he himself believes what he's saying.

"How do you think—" Eddie starts before Lisa cuts him off.

"He's right. *The Editor can only correct so much. The Author must end the story.* Those were the only words spoken in my vision. Lincoln must go. I'll stay to fight any danger that makes it past you."

Eddie shakes his head. "Wait, is that why you named me Eddie? Does anyone else see how cheesy this all is?"

Jennifer and Abby both snicker before Eddie continues. "Okay; whatever. So, it's me, Lincoln, Abby, Molly, and Taryn versus the Forces of Evil. I guess it's more fun to be the underdog."

Beth's eyes light up. "What about Jack?"

"Oh, yeah. You'll also have a ghost pirate named Jack on your side. I guess he's more a ghost *poet*, but still, he may be of some help." Lincoln tosses Eddie his cell phone, which still shows the photo of Jack that he showed Captain Merrick. "That's him."

"I feel much better now," Eddie quips as he tosses Lincoln's phone back. "Let's go; hopefully we can at least keep the element of surprise on our side."

Chapter 89

Everyone says their goodbyes and after a long hug with Noel, Lincoln leads them quietly past the seaside villas down the dark beach towards where he and Abby met Jophiel. With only the stars and moon lighting the way, they climb the rocks to the place where Jophiel's shack once stood, but find nothing but grass and a single coconut tree on the hill. Once everyone is atop the hill, Lincoln turns to Eddie.

"We should be able to see them approach from a ways off from up here. They'll head for Grace Bay— where the resorts are— coming from that direction."

Eddie stares out into the black abyss that is the Atlantic Ocean. Then he looks down to the far side of the hill where a cove sits, and follows the shoreline to a group of coconut trees about fifty yards from the water. "Abby, you'll stay here as a lookout. When you see the ship approaching, use your powers to force it into that cove, but make sure the entire crew makes it to land. The rest of us will take cover in that grove of coconut trees and attack them while they're are at their weakest."

Everyone nods and awaits further instruction, but Eddie just begins his dissent toward the grove.

"Then what?" Molly calls after him.

Eddie stops and turns back to the group. "Then we fight." He takes a few more steps and pauses again. "Molly, wait for the right time."

Chapter 90

"Why is Perry doing this, anyway?" Beth moans. "Why can't he just leave us all alone?"

Lisa sighs. "He won't rest until he's the most powerful being on Earth. Eddie, Lincoln, and now Molly, all have the ability to end him, so he'll do anything and everything to destroy them first."

Noel overhears the explanation and tears begin to form in her eyes. "Are my papa and Eddie in trouble? Like my mommy was?"

Jennifer is upon her and scoops Noel into her arms before Beth can even get up from the couch. "No, sweetie. Those bad people don't stand a chance against Eddie and your daddy. You just need to worry about what kind of delicious snack you want to order from room service. Okay?"

This brings a smile to Noel's face. "I know what I want already. Ice cream!!"

Beth grins, then playfully rolls her eyes. "Vanilla with sprinkles. It was Sara's favorite too. I'll call. Do you ladies want anything?"

Lisa grins. "Maybe a nibble on the delivery boy. Or girl."

Jennifer elbows her solidly in the ribs. "We'll have coffee."

Chapter 1

Abby sits alone atop the coconut tree on the hill-side, enjoying the clear night and the gentle breeze, until she spots the glowing sails of *The Bearded Ghost* off in the distance. She snaps her fingers, sending a flash of lightning across the sky— the agreed upon signal to warn the others of the ghost pirates' impending arrival. As the ship nears, Abby begins to wave her arms and a swirling wind starts to pick up. The sea becomes choppy and a heavy rain begins to fall. The angry screams of the pirates get closer and closer until the ship finally crashes into the rocky shoreline just beneath where Abby is perched on the tree.

Pirate after pirate jumps from the ship and makes their way to shore. Eddie signals for everyone to remain hidden until Perry becomes visible and the pirates begin to make their way closer to the grove. When the closest pirates are about twenty yards from the grove, Perry suddenly appears in their midst, his one remaining hand holding Captain Merrick's tightly.

Hey Lincoln, looks like you might have to kill your Eskimo brother.

Hey Eddie, did I make you this much of an asshole or did you pick that up since you've been here?

I can't remember being any other way, buddy. You ready to end this?

On your call.

Eddie takes a long drink from his flask and stands. "Attack!!". He sprouts his wings and launches himself into the air. As he surveys the scene from above, he feels an unfamiliar weight around his waist. A sword dangling from his side emits a bright white light. The sword inspires confidence; it's evident to Eddie that using it is how he can kill the ghost pirates. Why else would it have appeared? But as he looks around, he also sees just how terribly outnumbered they are. He watches Abby jump gracefully down from the hilltop and immediately knock half a dozen pirates over with a strong gust of wind. Perry and the Captain shift their attention from him to Lincoln, who is holding a few pirates at bay with a stick that he's using like a bo staff.

Unexpectedly decent skills with the bo staff, Lincoln.

Once Eddie is satisfied that Perry will stay and fight, he picks his targets.

Molly and Taryn are fighting back-to-back on one side of the beach while Lincoln and Abby are on the other. Eddie soars down toward the middle of the fray and unsheathes his sword. The sword is heavy, unlike the smaller swords that many of the pirates wield. He holds it tightly with two hands and swings it at the closest pirate just before landing safely at the edge of the water. He hears the screams of terror and it takes a moment to register that the screams are not coming from the pirate he struck, but from those who saw the sword find its mark. As he continues to find his targets, his victims sink into fiery pits as though they are being sent to their rightful place in hell.

A voice rings out. "It's the true death!"

"Get the sword," another voice calls out from behind him, and suddenly he's the sole focus of each and every pirate on the beach. They're on him quickly— too quickly for him to fly away— and it's everything he can do just to fend off their blows.

Abby tries to fight her way to his side, but she's grossly outnumbered; she can barely protect herself. She either doesn't have the time, or doesn't have the energy left to call on the weather to protect them.

Eddie catches a glimpse of Lincoln battling Captain Merrick and quickly scans the beach for the rest of his team before he sends two more pirates to damnation.

"Molly, now!" he yells as he scans the beach searching for the young vampire, but there's no sign of either

her or Taryn. Suddenly, he feels the blunt end of a club crash against the right side of his head. His vision goes in and out and an incessant ringing fills his head.

As he drops to his knees, across the beach Abby falls to the ground with a sword through her chest. Eddie reaches out for Abby and even though she is easily a hundred yards away, he could swear that he feels her hand grasp his. Before he can pull her to safety, the world goes black.

Chapter 92

Back at the condo there is a gentle knock on the door. "Room service," a pleasant voice calls out.

"Mmm, he sounds delicious," Lisa purrs.

"I better get the door." Beth pushes past her just in case Lisa isn't entirely joking.

Beth opens the door and then her horrified scream rings through the condo. Jennifer and Lisa are at her side in an instant. Perry stands at the door, teeth buried deep in the lifeless body of the room service attendant.

"You know, I'm full, and yet I know if I stop eating this I'll regret it." He removes his hand from the young man's back and the body drops to the ground with a sickening thud. "I know. Could I *be* any scarier?" He laughs as he looks into the eyes of the three women. "Now, where's the girl— the little one?"

Chapter 93

Eddie's vision begins to return, but all he can see at the moment is a blinding light. Music fills the air and for a moment he thinks that he's in Heaven, until he simultaneously feels every bruise that the ghost pirates put on his body.

"Is that Battle Hymn of the Republic?" he mumbles.

As more of his vision returns, he gazes upward where the sky has been ripped open and angelic warriors are pouring through the void and onto the beach. They're making quick work of the ghost pirates whose bodies are melting into fiery pits all over the cove.

Apparently, Abby pulled him out of harm's way. But where is she now?

Seemed like a fitting song to play for angels going into battle, no? The voice in his head was neither his own nor Lincoln's. It was a voice he had heard once before, but he could not place it.

What? Who is this?

It's me, silly. The portly angel playing the awesome trumpet. Some actually call me the Jimi Hendrix of

Trumpet, but He *calls me Jophiel. Pleasure to make your acquaintance, Eddie.*

Eddie nearly jumps out of his own skin when he notices the angel right behind him. It must have been Jophiel who pulled him to safety and not Abby.

Jophiel? Oh, uh, nice to meet you, too.

A third voice then enters Eddie's head.

Can we save the pleasantries for later? I could use a little help with the good captain here.

Eddie gets to his feet and scans the beach until he finally spots Lincoln, barely holding off Captain Merrick's thunderous sword strikes.

On my way, buddy.

Chapter 94

"Yeah, um, no," Lisa says as she freezes a two-foot-thick block of ice around Perry. "Go, now! Get them away from here. That won't hold him long." She pushes Jennifer, who already has Beth and Noel in her grasp, toward the door.

"Lisa, thank you." Jennifer hesitates like she has more that she wants to say.

"Run!" is all Lisa replies, before turning to find the block of ice empty.

"Lisa, baby, why's it gotta end like this? We were so alike, so fun-loving. Now you got your panties in a bunch all the time."

"*Hello*? *You* broke our bond, Perry," Lisa snaps back, the pain still evident in her voice. She takes two steps back, trying to keep enough distance between them to stay out of Perry's reach.

"And *you* were still hung up on Courtney. Jennifer and the slayer I can understand, but you two weren't even imprinted." The words have their desired effect as tears begin to form in Lisa's big blue eyes.

The Editor

"Yeah well, your bitch of a bride made sure to end any chance of reconciliation for Courtney and I."

"It's *Courtney and me* and watch your tongue; you've never been one to swear. You've always been the sweet, bubbly one. The one who wrote fun songs like *Smelly Bat*. Besides, then you killed her thereby killing a part of me and *forcing* me to break our bond. So, either we can continue to play the blame game until I tire of it and rip you apart, or, you can tell me where Jennifer took the child. And maybe, just maybe we can work on repairing that bond." Perry smiles at Lisa, seemingly sincerely, as he takes a step to close the distance between them.

"Hmmm. So, what you're saying is that you're using that good arm to extend an olive branch." She giggles. "No, hold on, I can do better. You want us to once again conquer the world *arm-in-arms*. If I agree, can we seal the deal with half a hug?"

"Ah, there's my fun-loving Lisa. I guess I haven't lost you after all." He takes another step forward and pins her against the wall.

"Okay, I'll tell you where they're headed, but only if you can give me ten." She bursts into laughter and holds both of her hands up in a high five position.

Perry's smile disappears and he bares his fangs.

His one hand is quickly around Lisa's throat, and he lifts her off the ground with ease.

"Okay, dear. Your humor has grown tiresome." He rips her head from her body and casually tosses it across the room. As her head hits against a wall, Lisa could swear that she saw Taryn holding Perry's hand before he could remove her heart from her torso.

Chapter 95

Eddie's heart pounds hard inside his chest as he grips his sword and soars across the beach, cutting down pirate after pirate on his way to Lincoln. He watches as Captain Merrick's sword snaps Lincoln's makeshift bo staff in two, knocking him to the ground.

Merrick places her boot on Lincoln's chest and raises her sword high above her head, ready to plunge it into his heart. She flashes a deadly smile. "If it makes you feel any better, Lincoln, you're a much better lover than you are a fighter."

Lincoln frowns. "Not really. And I wish I could say the same." He closes his eyes and thinks of how he has failed Noel as he waits for the sword to find its mark. The pain that he expects never comes. Instead, the air flows through his hair and the clank of metal on metal sounds more and more distant. He opens his eyes to see Captain Merrick's sword fly from her hand and Eddie's boot strike her ribs, knocking her to the ground. Their figures get smaller and smaller and he assumes that he's being carried to the afterlife, until he comes to an abrupt stop. He looks up to see Jennifer staring down at him.

Jennifer pauses a moment to catch her breath. "He's in the condo. Can you kill him?"

"Perry?" Lincoln's eyes grow wide as he feels for his ivory stake that is no longer in his jacket pocket. A lump forms in his throat. "Noel and Beth?"

"They're fine, thanks to Lisa. Now can you kill him?"

"My stake. It's gone and I don't know where I dropped it. Without ivory, I don't know how I'd kill him."

Jennifer looks around the resort in search of any hope, but is unable to find any.

"Chopsticks!" Lincoln suddenly shouts.

Jennifer stares back at him, hoping that he'll elaborate and that he hasn't just developed some weird form of Tourette's.

"The hibachi restaurant! Their decorations looked authentic and chopsticks are sometimes made from ivory. I could swear I saw—"

Before he can finish the sentence, Jennifer stands in front of them holding two chopsticks made of pure ivory. She grins from ear to ear. "Will these do?"

Chapter 96

Taryn grabs Perry calmly and confidently by the hand.

Perry turns quickly, but as he gazes upon the woman before him, his face softens. "Janice?" Perry asks softly, in disbelief.

"Yes, Perbear."

"But... how?" Perry asks, trying to blink away the image of his fictional wife who died a human many years ago.

"You're better than this, Perry. You don't really want to hurt these people," Janice says before Taryn momentarily loses control and reveals a glimpse of herself to Perry. She quickly channels Janice again.

"What is this witchcraft!?" Perry demands, grabbing Janice by the neck. "Who are you really!?"

"It's me, Perbear," she chokes out, desperately clawing at his hand and gasping for air.

Perry can't understand how this witch could know about Janice, let alone know about the pet name that she had for him.

"Janice is dead...or never lived. Whatever." Perry closes his eyes tightly and shakes his head again, hoping that the image of Janice wouldn't be there when he reopened them.

"YOU are a heartless tramp who obviously has poor taste in literature," he says, coming to the conclusion that she must be a fan of Lincoln's lesser works. He squeezes his grip tighter as if trying to pop a water balloon and begins to laugh maniacally. "Maybe you'll meet the *real* Janice in the afterlife."

"NOOOO!" Molly makes it to the door and peers into the condo where Perry has a woman firmly in his grasp. Suddenly, the unfamiliar woman morphs into Taryn. Her scream causes Perry to loosen his grip momentarily and Taryn begins to fall, but never hits the ground.

Chapter 97

Eddie stares at the spot where Lincoln was just a moment before and fears the worst, thinking Perry may have teleported in and taken him.

Lincoln? What happened?

I'm okay. Jennifer—

Lincoln's reply is interrupted by a surprisingly strong kick to Eddie's ribs from Captain Merrick. Eddie drops his sword and doubles over in agony. He recovers fast enough to block Merrick's second kick and two punches.

"I like a woman who doesn't give up." He grins as he catches her next blow and easily twists her arm behind her back.

"I like a man who does." Merrick drives her boot heel into the top of his foot. He screams in pain and releases her. She grabs his sword, but is unfamiliar with using a heavier sword and attempts to swing it wildly with one hand.

Eddie steps in, blocking her arm and missing most of the blow. He knees her in the stomach and she drops the sword, falling to her knees.

"Well done." There's a hint of relief in her voice. "Send me home quickly, is all I ask. One captain to another."

Eddie knows that he must, but he can't bring himself to actually do it.

Abby— who was finally able to remove the sword from her chest— slowly makes her way toward them. "Here. I'll do it." She reaches for the sword.

Captain Merrick scoffs. "At least give me the honor of dying by a true warrior's hand, not some wench that was run through by one of me deckhands."

Abby snaps her fingers and a mini bolt of lightning strikes the captain, knocking her on her face.

"The sword only works in my hands. Or in one of the angels.'" Eddie looks down the beach, then into the sky where the angels are disappearing one by one. Jophiel gives him a nod and a soldier's salute before blaring one last verse of *Battle Hymn of the Republic* and disappearing back into the Heavens himself.

Captain Merrick gets back to her knees and grins. Eddie levels the sword with her breastbone and his hands begin to shake.

"It's time." Captain Merrick quickly grips half way down the blade and runs it into her own heart before melting into a fiery pit at Eddie's feet.

The Editor

"That never gets old." Abby grins at Eddie, who stands there in shock. "Well, I guess we should head back to check on everyone else. Perry is still out there somewhere." She starts to head back in the direction of the condo.

Suddenly, a glowing body appears from behind a coconut tree, right behind Abby.

"Abby, look out!" Eddie raises his sword and begins to charge at the pirate.

Abby whirls around and grabs the pirate just in time to pull him out of the way of Eddie's blade. "Eddie! Eddie! Stop! It's okay. This is Jack." She turns the pirate so that Eddie can get a good look at him. "Jack meet Eddie."

Eddie slowly sheaths his sword and extends Jack a hand. "Well, what *are* we going to do with you?"

Abby continues toward the condo, picking up her pace to an injured vampire jog, which is equivalent to an Olympic sprinter's run. "Let's worry about that *after* we kill Perry," she calls back.

Chapter 98

Jennifer races back to the condo carrying Lincoln as if he were a small child.

As they approach, they see the condo door is wide open. Lincoln's stomach drops. Jennifer carries him across the apartment threshold but then freezes dead in her tracks and the change in momentum makes Lincoln fly from her arms onto the floor where he smacks his head against the bottom of the kitchen island.

"Damnit, Jennifer! What was that?" He turns and scowls at her before noticing that she isn't moving. He scans the room and none of the vampires are moving except Molly, who is slowly crawling toward Perry. "Molly? Are you okay?"

"Can't... hold it... much... longer," she whispers, now clawing at Perry's feet.

Lincoln swallows hard and reaches for the chopsticks in his pocket. He makes his way to the monster, hoping the ivory in the chopsticks will be enough to end this mess.

The Editor

He stands face-to-face with what was once one of his most ridiculous literary creations— now brought to life. He stares into Perry's hollow eyes and vows to himself that from this point on he'll write deeper characters and happier stories. Then Molly gasps and the hollow eyes staring back at him blink.

Reflexively, his right arm shoots out and the first chopstick finds its way through Perry's left eye.

Perry falls to his knees and grasps at Lincoln's waist. "I can't... I can't..."

Jennifer shrieks as Molly's effect wears off and she gazes upon the horror in front of her.

Lincoln kicks Perry in the chest, knocking him backwards before one of his claws can do any damage. Then he takes the other chopstick and plunges it awkwardly into Perry's chest, praying that it finds its target.

Abby gets to the doorway just in time to see Perry's right eye grow large. Then his entire body begins to tremor and dissolves into a pile of ash at Lincoln's feet.

Chapter 99

Eddie pushes through the doorway with Jack close behind. He rushes to Lincoln's side.

"Is that?" Eddie asks, but Lincoln remains silent.

"Yeah, that was Perry."

The voice sounds like Lisa's and Eddie glances to his right where her disembodied head is speaking.

He nearly jumps through the ceiling. "Whoa! What in the—"

"Would somebody mind placing my head back on my torso so that I can heal properly?"

"Now thur's something that ye don't see every day." Jack's glowing eyes grow wider. Everyone notices him for the first time since he entered the room.

Jennifer's brow furrows. She looks from Jack to Eddie. "So, did we not get rid—"

"All but Jack," Abby interrupts as she steps between Jack and Jennifer. "I don't see any reason why we need to kill him."

Jack smiles warmly and places a hand on Abby's shoulder. "Thank you, Abigail, but I'm fine with whatever fate ye may decide for me."

The Editor

Everyone turns to Eddie, who then nudges Lincoln. "What do you wanna do with the helpful pirate?"

Lincoln continues to stare at the pile of ash at his feet, but half-heartedly addresses Jack. "What would you do if we let you go, Jack?"

Jack hesitates. "Well, I guess I'd get back aboard *The Bearded Ghost* and sail the seven seas, searching for inspiration for me poetry."

"How would you sail without a crew?" Eddie asks.

Jack laughs. "She sails herself. Plus, if I run into any danger, we'll be back again the next day— unless of course that danger be of your variety." He nods toward the sword that still hangs from Eddie's waist.

"Sailing actually sounds nice." Abby stares at a painting of a sailboat that hangs slightly askew after the commotion in the suite. "Maybe Beth and I can tag along for a bit?"

"Beth and Noel!" Lincoln gasps. "Where—"

"Easy, Lincoln. I dropped them off at the diner in the middle of the resort for a milkshake. It was the most crowded place available at this hour. Let's just take a minute to celebrate our victory. They're fine," Jennifer reassures him.

"Just the same, I'd like to see them myself. Let's go. Jack, you're free to go. Don't make me regret it."

Jack nods. "Abigail, I'll stay docked for an hour. If you'd like to join me, you know where to find me ship. If not, I hope our paths will meet again. The same goes for the rest of ya. It's been a pleasure fightin' on the side of good for once." Jack bows before grabbing a recently restocked bottle of rum and leaving the condo.

Lincoln pushes past everyone with Eddie close behind. They leave the condo, headed straight for the diner.

What's with you, Lincoln?

It was too easy. Killing Perry.

Oh, you'd have preferred more of a challenge? Maybe you should write more bad-ass villains, then.

No, that's not what I mean. It just doesn't feel... over.

It's probably just your adrenaline dropping back to normal coupled with the fact that you killed a vampire with... were those chopsticks I saw in the ash?

Maybe you're right. I'll calm down when I'm holding my daughter in my arms.

Fair enough. Is that the diner?

Chapter 100

Before they even enter the diner, Eddie can tell that something is wrong. He can smell the blood.

"Lincoln, don't," Eddie reaches for him, but it's too late.

Lincoln frantically pushes through the diner doors and stops abruptly, adjusting to the horrifying scene in front of him. Eddie stumbles in behind him and sees the blood. Large puddles cover most of the once black and white checkered floor. Eddie holds up a hand, motioning for Jennifer to keep Abby and Lisa outside, but it's ignored.

Lincoln is sobbing uncontrollably, going from body to body searching for any signs of life. Eddie fights the urge to vomit as he and the others begin to help, turning over body after mangled body. But there's no sign of Beth or Noel.

"What did this?" Jennifer half whispers, half whimpers.

Lisa bends down to examine a body more closely. "The bite marks look animalistic."

"Lincoln, they're not here." Eddie tries to sound optimistic, but then a banging sound coming from behind the diner counter puts everyone on guard.

Eddie draws his sword and sprouts his wings to get an aerial view of whatever danger lurks behind the counter, but when he gets up high enough to get a view, there's nothing but a few broken plates scattered on the floor. The banging sound begins again. Then sounds of crying.

"Papa! Is that you? Help! Please."

Lincoln scampers to his feet and dives over the counter cutting himself on the broken plates. The crying is coming from inside a locked cabinet. Lincoln uses a broomstick to pry the cupboard open and Noel leaps into his arms. "Papa! Papa! It was horrible," she sobs. Lincoln buries her face in his chest and takes her out of the diner as quickly as possible.

"It's okay, baby doll. You're safe now."

Chapter 101

"Lincoln, Beth is still missing, damnit! You have to ask her what she saw," Abby argues, fangs bared. Eddie stands between her and Lincoln.

"Abby, I will, but give her a second; she's in shock." Lincoln tries to speak softly enough that Noel can't hear them in the other room. But sure enough, the door opens and Jennifer emerges with Noel in her arms.

"Every second we waste brings Beth closer to death." Tears begin to fill Abby's beautiful vampire eyes.

"It's okay, Papa. We need to save Aunt Beth. I can be brave."

Jennifer hands Noel to Lincoln who takes her in his bandaged hands, and sits her on his lap on the couch. Jennifer sits between them and Eddie. Abby and Lisa sit down in chairs across the room. Molly and Taryn stay at the table, but close enough that they can hear.

"Alright, sweetheart." Lincoln squeezes his daughter tight against his chest. "Just do your best to tell us exactly what happened, okay?"

Noel smiles bravely, but the horror is evident in her eyes when she thinks back to what happened.

"We were drinking our milkshakes. I had strawberry and Aunt Beth had chocolate mixed with strawberry and we were talking to Cookie— he was the nice man who made the milkshakes. He was gonna get me a cookie— which is funny because his name is Cookie. But then we heard a roar. Then, outside, the biggest cat I ever saw was scratching at the door and it looked mad."

"There's no jungle cats on this island, are there?" Jennifer asks.

Lincoln shakes his head. "Not in the wild." He pats Noel on her knee. "Go on, sweetheart."

Noel pauses, as if trying to remember where she had left off. "Oh, yeah. So, we were all screaming— even Cookie— but he was brave and he ran to lock the doors." Noel stops and closes her eyes.

"Did he not make it, honey?" Abby pries.

Noel opens her eyes suddenly. "No, he made it, but then the man that was with the cat just walked through the door, grabbed Cookie and threw him behind the counter. He opened the door and a pretty woman flew in. I ran back to check on Cookie and he opened the cupboard, pushed me inside, shut the door, and then

I just heard the roaring and the screaming." Tears stream down her sunburned cheeks.

"Jack did this?" Abby asks angrily.

Noel tilts her head to the side and looks at Abby. "Huh? No, not Mr. Jack. This man was not a nice man like Mr. Jack."

Abby turns to Lincoln and Eddie. "I don't understand. We killed the rest of the ghost pirates."

Eddie glances at Molly before speaking. "It wasn't a pirate."

"Adam," Molly gasps. If Jennifer wasn't so insanely fast, Molly would've made it out the door.

Jennifer shoves Molly back down onto a chair. "Sit down, Molly! You need blood, and even with a full stomach, you aren't fighting him alone."

Molly doesn't protest, but the fire in her eyes is long from gone.

Abby turns to Lincoln. "Do you think the flying woman was Riley?"

"Taryn, would you mind taking Noel in to bed and singing her an Irish lullaby? Maybe let her mom give her a kiss goodnight? I'll be in shortly." Lincoln speaks slowly and softly, trying not to betray the absolute terror that he feels inside.

Taryn nods and smiles. She walks over and takes

Noel by her small hand, guiding her gracefully into the bedroom.

"Lincoln, what's wrong?" Abby's voice shakes.

"Yeah, Adam, and Riley for that matter, are completely beatable," Jennifer reassures him.

Lisa stares into Lincoln's eyes. "It's not Adam or Riley that troubles him. The cat was in my vision."

Lincoln hangs his head. "The cat is part of a story a hundred times as terrifying as yours. Its master makes Perry and the ghost pirates look like characters from a children's book." Lincoln slowly makes his way to the kitchen. He returns and hands Eddie a bottle of bourbon. "Remember that *more badass villain* you asked for? Well, drink up, buddy. She's here."

Acknowledgements

Thank you to the love of my life, Ashley. Your support allows me to chase this crazy dream and means everything to me. You, Larkin, and Lincoln are the driving forces behind all that I do. Thank you to my Mom. You taught me to dream and to be creative. You also read to me when I was too lazy to read to myself. Thank you to my brother, Brett. You always read the crappiest versions of my novels and support me nonetheless. I sincerely appreciate it. I love you all.

Steve, thank you for validating me as a writer. Noah, thank you. You definitely helped my writing and boosted my confidence. Sarah, thank you for believing in my story and for the tedious editing. It's truly been a pleasure working with you. Jordan, thank you for your patience working with me on the cover. It turned out great!

Thank you to all my friends and family and to the community of Uniontown. Your support thus far has been overwhelming and very much appreciated.

About the Author

Luke Carroll makes his home in cozy Uniontown, PA with his gorgeous wife of eleven years and their two incredible daughters. When he's not reading or writing, he's usually selling drugs (legally), coaching a soccer team, attempting to master the art of Tang Soo Do, or trying to keep his DVR from hitting maximum capacity.

Luke is a dreamer, or so he's been told, and that aids him in his ability to write urban fantasy novels. He likes to laugh, so he selfishly sprinkles things that make him chuckle throughout each book. He prides himself on being able to weave God and a positive message into even the most twisted of stories. He also enjoys putting his own unique spin on a well-known story until it is barely recognizable.

You can read more about his works in progress along with a bevy of other incredibly important information on his blog at www.lukecarroll.com

Visit us at:

www.antcolonypress.com

www.facebook.com/antcolonypress

When Shadows Creep by K. Brooks

The Darkness comes, slinking out of the shadows in Flynn's new home, Freemont House. With Flynn's life in danger, his adoptive tribe—the other centuries-old Guardians—will do whatever it takes to bring him home. He reluctantly sheds the autonomy of his life by the sea and returns to Caldwell Manor, but the Darkness follows him, and threatens to unravel the Guardians' very existence.

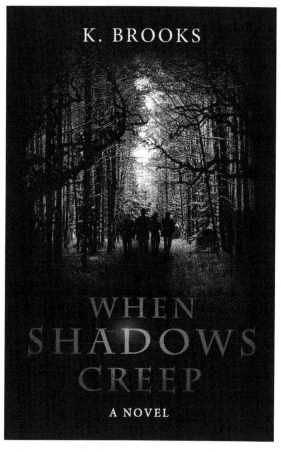

www.antcolonypress.com

Unconventional by Scarlet Birch

Sam isn't supposed to be in love with Louis. She likes him. What they have is fine. But Love? When he drops the L word, she won't say it back, and she may lose Louis—the only constant thing in her life—forever. He won't give up on her, though, and as her life falls apart he is the foundation she didn't know she needed.

www.antcolonypress.com

In The House Of In Between by JD Buffington

Phoebe Backlund, who built her family's dream home, has no explanation for the events that take place there. She invites curious thrill seekers and notorious skeptics alike in the golden age of spiritualism to experience the house's clockwork poltergeists. Knocks, slamming doors, screams, and looming specters delight and terrify her guests, but answers are as elusive as the phantoms.

www.antcolonypress.com

Made in the USA
San Bernardino, CA
28 September 2018